"We simply can't keep you on."

"Not at all?"

Caden straightened. "I wish we could. But now's really not a good time."

It would be challenging enough to keep the vet clinic afloat and alleviate community concern regarding Dr. Wallow's death.

Stephanie's gaze faltered. "But what about the agreement we signed?"

He tensed. "The what?"

"Dr. Wallow had me sign a bunch of papers. I have copies."

He rubbed the back of his neck. "I see. Can you give me a moment to review those documents?"

Chewing on her bottom lip, she nodded. She looked on the verge of tears, making Caden feel like a jerk for even having this conversation.

He flipped back to her internship application. He recognized the address. "You're staying with the Herrons?"

She nodded.

He studied her. Was there a story behind that? The women the older couple took in always had one. While he wasn't one to assume the worst, he also needed to stay alert. If his ex-fiancée had taught him anything, it was that a selfish conniver could hide behind a beautiful and seemingly kind and benevolent smile.

Jennifer Slattery is a writer and speaker who has addressed women's and church groups across the nation. As the founder of Wholly Loved Ministries, she and her team help women rest in their true worth and live with maximum impact. When not writing, Jennifer loves spending time with her adult daughter and hilarious husband. Visit her online at jenniferslatterylivesoutloud.com to learn more or to book her for your next women's event.

Books by Jennifer Slattery

Love Inspired

Restoring Her Faith
Hometown Healing
Building a Family
Chasing Her Dream
Her Small-Town Refuge

Visit the Author Profile page at LoveInspired.com.

Her Small-Town Refuge

Jennifer Slattery

LOVE INSPIRED
INSPIRATIONAL ROMANCE

LOVE INSPIRED®
INSPIRATIONAL ROMANCE

Recycling programs
for this product may
not exist in your area.

ISBN-13: 978-1-335-75908-5

Her Small-Town Refuge

Love Inspired
22 Adelaide St. West, 41st Floor
Toronto, Ontario M5H 4E3, Canada
www.LoveInspired.com

Printed in U.S.A.

The Spirit of the Lord is upon me, because he hath anointed me to preach the gospel to the poor; he hath sent me to heal the brokenhearted, to preach deliverance to the captives, and recovering of sight to the blind, to set at liberty them that are bruised.
—*Luke* 4:18

Dedicated to all abuse survivors
who have courageously sought refuge
and healing. God sees you, knows you,
goes before you and will never leave you.

Chapter One

Stephanie's stomach tightened as she studied her reflection in the mirror. Had she made the right decision coming to Sage Creek, Texas? Uprooting her daughter for an internship that could easily lead to nothing?

She took a deep breath and faced her three-year-old daughter, who sat singing on the bed behind her. Everyone said, with her long black hair and pale blue eyes, that she was a miniature Stephanie.

She smoothed a hand over Maddy's soft locks. "That's quite a tune."

Stephanie would do anything in her power to keep her daughter so carefree. They were safe, thanks to the address protection program and the thousands of miles separating them from her abusive ex-husband. Although he'd soon be released from prison, he'd never find her and Maddy.

She thought back to the night he'd been arrested. Learning he'd killed a man in a bar fight, knowing she could be next, had given her the courage to finally leave.

Next step? Turning her internship into full-time employment.

She needed to make a great first impression—professional and determined but cooperative. Competent but teachable, conscientious yet friendly and relaxed.

A knock sounded on her bedroom door.

Stephanie scooped Maddy up and balanced her on her hip. "Come in."

Cassandra Herron, the woman who'd so kindly opened her home, free of charge, poked her head in. "Breakfast's ready." Her grandmotherly appearance—silver hair that reached just below her ears and huggably plump frame—had a way of instantly decreasing Stephanie's anxiety.

But then, after breakfast, as everyone migrated from the kitchen table and Stephanie prepared to leave, Maddy clung to her. Regardless of how well-screened the Herrons were, they were still largely strangers. And Maddy had already endured so much transition. If only Stephanie could spend some unhurried time cuddling her on the couch, reading her favorite story.

She couldn't help but feel as if she were abandoning her precious girl.

"Now, now, there's nothing to fuss about." Cassandra whisked the crying child off to the living room to read a story.

"I know all this hasn't been easy." Her husband, Vincent Herron, a kind man who spent most of his time tending their orchard, placed his coffee mug in the sink. "But you did the right thing coming here. For yourself and your daughter."

"Thanks."

His words bolstered her courage as she told her precious little one goodbye, climbed into her car and headed to her first day of work.

She arrived to find two vehicles, one a black extended cab pickup with mud caked along the bottom rim and the other an older red compact. Sitting in the parking lot facing the vet's office, she watched a man through the window. His white lab coat and jeans, and the way he was bustling about, suggested he was the partner Dr. Wallow had mentioned. He had sandy brown hair, was well-built, maybe six foot one. He was talking with a much shorter woman whom Stephanie assumed was the receptionist.

A knock on her side window startled her. She turned to see an older woman with big poufy blond hair and mascara-clumped lashes staring back at her.

Stephanie lowered her window. "Hello?"

"Hi, sugar. Think you can help me out here? I've got some feral cats I brought in to get spayed and neutered. Doing my part, you know? But seeing how's I'm outnumbered and all…" She laughed and fluffed her bouffant hair.

"Um… Yeah, okay." Stephanie gathered her things and stepped out into the humid Texas air. Not quite seven thirty, and it felt like the temperature was already topping eighty. Not that she was surprised, it being mid-June and all.

Locking her car, Stephanie followed the woman to her vehicle and the four cat carriers on the ground nearby.

"You grab those two." The woman jerked her head toward the left and reached for the containers on the right. "I've got these."

Stephanie complied and, carting a meowing feline in each hand, trailed the woman into her new employment. This wasn't the kind of entrance she wanted to make on her first day, though hopefully her boss would appreciate her kindness.

As she entered the facility a blast of cool air swept over her, carrying with it the faint scent of disinfectant and lavender. The man in the lab coat turned toward her, his tight expression smoothing into a formal smile. Stephanie recognized him from the clinic's website. A dusting of whiskers covered his square jaw, and he wore his sandy brown hair shorter on the sides.

He stood nearly a foot taller than her five-foot-four self.

"Hello." When his eyes, green with brown radiating from the pupils, landed on hers, her breath hitched.

"Hi."

He looked from her to the other women to the carriers, then back to her. "Ma'am, how can I help you?"

The lady rushed forward and deposited her kennels on the counter with a thud, knocking over a canister of pens. "I found these poor critters in my daughter's backyard. I'm pretty sure there's a slew more of them hiding out in the bushes."

The receptionist, a middle-aged woman with a pointed chin and short, slightly frizzy hair, hurried to tidy up fallen items.

"I'm Dr. Caden Stoughton." He eyed an orange-and-white splotched cat that was meowing pitifully. "Are they ill?"

The woman frowned. "I don't rightly know, although I wouldn't be surprised. But I don't have money for none of that. Barely got the eighty dollars to get them fixed up so they can't have no more babies."

Stephanie set her carriers on the ground, then inched back, listening to the woman go on and on about some deal her local vet offered, one Dr. Stoughton clearly had no intention of matching.

If the other place offered such great rates, why had she come here?

"Ma'am?" The receptionist diverted Stephanie's attention. "You two together?"

"Huh?" She glanced from the vet to the woman, then back to the man. "Oh, no. I'm Stephanie Thornton, the intern from Santa Ana, California."

The receptionist frowned. "I see." She stood and approached the doctor. "Sir, can I interrupt a moment?"

"Of course." He offered the cat woman a taut smile. "Would you excuse me for a moment?"

The lady rolled her eyes. "Don't bother. I'll take these poor creatures to the mobile vet I saw driving about downtown the other day."

Stoughton visibly stiffened. Did the mention of the other vet upset him, or was it the fact that a potential client was displeased and leaving?

The woman muttered something about a two-for-one deal and vets who cared more about animals than money and stormed out lugging half of her carriers with her.

"Hello, Ms....?"

"Stephanie Thornton." She repeated what she'd told his receptionist. Unfortunately, his tense expression didn't send a warm welcome.

"Dr. Wallow—" he swallowed, and his eyes grew misty "—isn't with us anymore."

"I see." Had he switched clinics? Surely he would've told her. Besides, as far as she knew this was the only one in Sage Creek. "Where can I find him?"

"No, dear." The receptionist deposited a pencil in the holder. "What he means is, he died. Brain aneurysm. We just found out about it."

Her gaze shot back and forth between them. "Oh, my. I'm so very sorry."

"As you can imagine, things are pretty chaotic for us right now." Sorrow lengthened his expression.

"I understand." Lost wages aside, that would give her and Maddy more time to get settled. "Would you like to delay my start date?"

The phone started ringing as yet another client entered, an older woman who appeared deeply distraught. Wallow's death had hit this community hard. She almost felt guilty for talking about her internship, but she felt equally uncomfortable hanging around with nothing to do. Nor could she simply leave.

Dr. Stoughton raked a hand through his hair and looked

from Stephanie to the crowded lobby, then back to her. "I'm sorry, but I can't have this conversation right now." He hurried to greet the older woman, who almost immediately began to sob. He appeared to stiffen for a moment, as if unsure of what to do, but then offered her a somewhat awkward embrace.

The poor guy had to be on emotional overload.

"Don't worry, sweetie." The receptionist placed a hand on Stephanie's arm. "It's not you. But you have to know you couldn't have picked a worse day to come prancing in here."

Stephanie blinked and took a step back. She knew she'd face some adjustments, moving to a small town and merging with an established, most likely tight-knit work culture. She'd even anticipated potentially snarky coworkers. But...

Most likely all the tension she felt stemmed from their grief. Hopefully, once things settled down, he'd come to see her as an asset rather than an intrusion.

In the meantime...? She supposed the best thing she could do was try to learn whatever she could while staying out of Dr. Stoughton's way.

She grabbed a chair from the far end of the desk and pulled it next to his receptionist. "Um, mind if I sit here and just kind of watch you, ma'am?"

She eyed her for a moment, then shrugged. "So long as you realize I don't got time to babysit you or nothing. And call me Lisa."

Babysit? Tears pricked Stephanie's eyes. She blinked them away. "Of course."

She spent the rest of the morning watching Lisa attempt to shift appointments in between answering the incessantly ringing phone while the doctor spent most of his time consoling grieving clients and the numerous community members who popped in.

Dr. Wallow had clearly made an impact on people. She would've loved the chance to train under him.

At least he'd wanted her here. She wasn't sure Dr. Staughton felt the same.

Taking a moment to catch his breath, Caden shifted to watch Stephanie Thornton. Sitting, stiff and maybe even a little jumpy, beside Lisa, the poor woman looked like a newborn kitten caught in the rooster's coop. She probably regretted being here at all, which he could completely understand.

Surely she'd recognize why she couldn't stay. If she were coming on as fully trained and experienced staff, that would be one thing. But a new-to-the-field intern?

There was no way.

He hadn't even had time to process Wallow's death, the man who'd been his mentor, something of a second dad, and a dear friend. Laughing and joking Friday. Then, just like that, gone.

The clinic doors dinged open, and a twentysomething girl entered tugging on what looked to be a pit-Labrador mix. Based on the muscly dog's resistance, Caden needed to gear up for a challenging exam. And help the fella calm down as quickly as possible. One hyped-up patient could easily rile up every other animal in the clinic. Thankfully, the big boy wore a muzzle.

"Oh!" Stephanie was at Caden's side in an instant. "How can I—" She flinched as the pit-Lab mix let out an odd bellowing sound and lunged toward a tan Pomeranian sniffing about her owner's feet.

The lobby erupted into a ruckus of barks, growls, gasps and the commands of pet owners as they fought to quiet or shield their animals.

As if their day hadn't been hectic enough.

He glanced at Lisa, who was once again on the phone.

Why hadn't she prepared him for such an uncontrollable patient? Better yet, why hadn't she rescheduled? Then again, maybe she'd tried. Nearly half of her calls had led to voice mail.

He glanced about, weighing options. "Let's hurry and get this big boy into an exam room."

Stephanie nodded, and after a significant struggle, the four of them—Caden, Stephanie, the dog and owner—gathered in the nearest vacant room.

He motioned toward the chair along the wall and offered what he hoped to be a soothing smile.

Stephanie stood to the right of the door, picking at her pinkie nail. But then she slid to the floor, maintaining distance between her and the dog, probably so as not to scare him further. As if watching his cues.

"You're okay." She said that a few times in a soft, soothing voice.

Evidence of training or intuition? Either way, he appreciated her quick response. The clinic could really benefit from such skills, in their present chaotic environment especially. If he had the time to work with her, which he didn't. And considering he'd probably have to cut their appointments by half, he doubted they had funds to pay her. He'd be lucky to hold on to his current staff.

Caden sat on the ground, maintaining a slack, nonthreatening posture. He introduced himself to the owner, a young lady named Aislyn. "Would he—what's his name?"

"Bubba," the girl said.

"Would Bubba like a treat?"

She released a breath. "I think that would help."

He rose slowly and reached into the glass jar behind him, intentionally clinking the biscuits before retrieving one. He held the beef-flavored snack out in his open palm. When the dog made no move to take it, he dropped it onto the ground, then slid it toward him.

After some timid sniffs, Bubba ate it, which hopefully helped increase his trust.

With the treat gone, Stephanie, still speaking soothingly, reached out and let the dog sniff the back of her hand. He growled, pulled back, then sniffed again.

The fluorescent lighting shimmered off her long, silky black hair, her blue eyes radiating compassion. The gentleness she displayed made her all the more beautiful.

Distractingly beautiful.

Caden cleared his throat. "Stephanie, why don't you grab this fella's chart from Lisa." Then to the owner, "When was he last in?"

"This is our first time here."

"I see." In other words, he could have all sorts of behavioral problems. Problems Caden normally wouldn't avoid. But today was anything but normal.

Nearly half an hour later, the dog was as calm as a Lab lazing in the sun, largely thanks to Stephanie. She seemed to have an almost instinctive ability to soothe the dog and draw him in. That could be super helpful in this line of work. He could understand why Dr. Wallow had invited her in. Under normal circumstances, he might be inclined to let her stay.

The clinic probably wouldn't return to normal for some time.

Normal without Wallow? An ache filled his chest.

He shook the thought aside and refocused on examining his patient. The poor guy didn't like his head touched, and Caden soon discovered why. Bubba had a double ear infection. Thankfully, his eardrums hadn't shattered. "You made the right choice by bringing him in. A week's worth of antibiotics and a prescription to help with pain and he'll be good to go."

"Thank you, Doctor." The girl stood, her wide smile producing twin dimples on each cheek.

"Of course." He dashed out, grabbed the appropriate medication, then returned to explain. "Give us a call if you have any problems." He held the door open for her, then paused, thinking of all the ruckus he'd created in the lobby. "And, um... How about you take him out through the back. Get him settled in your car, then return to pay the bill."

She laughed. "Good idea."

He and Stephanie walked Aislyn and her dog out. Once the door clicked closed, Stephanie released an audible sigh.

Caden chuckled. "Quite a day, huh?"

Her shy smile accentuated her beauty. "You could say that." She straightened and tucked her hair behind her ears. "But nothing I can't handle."

Her eager professionalism demonstrated how important this position was to her. A thought that only made what he needed to do harder.

Lisa poked her head into the hall. "Hey, Doc? Mrs. Ellis is on the phone, and she's really upset. I know you're busy, but she insists on talking with you."

He sighed and nodded. Dr. Wallow had not only cared for all three of the woman's dogs, but after the death of her husband, he'd periodically popped in on her, more frequently as she aged. That might be another area Caden needed to step into.

"I'll take the call in my office."

He was never very good at these types of conversations, and the numerous calls he'd already held hadn't improved his skills.

Sometimes words were insufficient, but he offered a prayer and did his best. After hanging up, he sat behind his desk for a moment, trying to focus his foggy and scattered brain when what he really wanted to do was head home to sit on his porch with his dogs. But he had a practice to save.

When he returned to the lobby, he found Stephanie sitting in the chair she'd pulled beside Lisa's desk.

Had she flown here? If so, what would it cost to catch an earlier flight home? Regardless, he'd pay it. That was the ethical thing to do.

He scanned the busy lobby, filled with more clients than he could possibly get to before the clinic closed. With how incessantly the phone had been ringing and all of Lisa's appointment-shifting, his schedule wasn't likely to lighten anytime soon.

He'd be smart to thin down their patient list, only that would cut their income. The only solution was to hire another veterinarian.

That meant placing ads, screening résumés and hosting interviews.

And hoping he found someone halfway decent.

"Stephanie?" He caught her eye, trying to ignore the vulnerability radiating from her. "Can we talk in my office for a minute?"

The poor woman likely had numerous hopes tied to this internship, as he had years ago when he'd stood in her place. But cutting her loose was the right thing to do, for the clinic and her.

"Yes, of course." She grabbed a pocket notebook and pen and sprang to her feet.

He glanced at the first page, filled with notes neatly written in small, precise lettering. An indication of how eager she was to be here and to learn?

And here he was, about to be a dream killer.

Suppressing a sigh, he led Stephanie down the hall and into his office, keeping the door open.

"Please." He swept a hand toward the metal folding chair in front of his desk, then sat across from her. "As you've seen, things are quite chaotic around here, and with Dr. Wallow gone…"

He glanced toward his former colleague's desk lining the opposite wall, feeling the weight of its emptiness. This place wouldn't be the same without him. Sorrow tightened his throat. He cleared it, refocusing on the beautiful woman anxiously waiting for him to finish his thought.

He shifted. "I do apologize for your less-than-welcoming welcome."

She offered a timid smile. "I completely understand." Her face sobered. "And I'm really sorry for your loss."

"I appreciate that." An awkward silence stretched between them. "I hate to say this, I really do, but we simply can't keep you on."

"At all?"

Did her question imply she was open to part time? Could he handle that? Planning training opportunities, teaching through procedures, giving her the time and attention an intern deserved?

No. He had way too many other things to focus on.

He straightened. "I wish we could. But now's really not a good time."

It would be challenging enough to keep the place afloat and alleviate community concern regarding Dr. Wallow's death. Seemed a good number of folks placed their faith in him more than the clinic. Would their practice lose yet more clients to that fancier, more modern clinic one town over?

Her gaze faltered. "But what about the agreement we signed?"

He tensed. "The what?"

"Dr. Wallow had me sign a bunch of papers. I have copies."

Great. Just when he thought this day couldn't become any more complicated.

He rubbed the back of his neck. "I see. Can you give me a moment to review those documents?"

Chewing on her bottom lip, she nodded. She looked on the verge of tears, making Caden feel like a jerk for even having this conversation.

He stood, crossed the room to the rusted pea-green filing cabinet and rummaged through the bottom drawer. He located Stephanie's papers easily and quickly scanned through them. She was right. They'd signed a formal agreement that included her terms and pay. While her salary wasn't much more than minimum wage, it'd still pose a challenge.

Most likely for her as well, even with Sage Creek's low cost of living.

He flipped back to her internship application. He recognized the address. "You're staying with the Herrons?"

She nodded.

He studied her. Was there a story behind that? The ladies the older couple took in always had one. While he wasn't one to assume the worst, he also needed to stay alert. If his ex-fiancée had taught him anything it was that a selfish conniver could hide behind a beautiful and seemingly kind and benevolent smile.

Chapter Two

Stephanie returned to the Herrons' orchard mentally and emotionally exhausted and fighting the beginnings of a tension headache. Her first day hadn't gone anything like she'd hoped, and her conversation with Dr. Stoughton had only heightened her insecurities.

Her mom had tried to talk her out of coming here. She'd wanted them to move in with her. But Stephanie had felt so certain this internship would lead to more.

What if she'd been wrong?

Contractually, could Dr. Stoughton let her go? He sure acted like he wanted to.

She sighed and rubbed her face. She'd spent nearly all she had just getting out here. Besides, Maddy had experienced enough transitions in her short life. Stephanie wouldn't uproot her again.

Tears pricked her eyes, but crying wouldn't help her any. She took in a few deep breaths to center herself. She'd come a long way, in distance and effort. Some might call her actions reckless, but she needed this to work.

The front door of the Herrons' two-story farmhouse flew open and Maddy dashed out. Her shiny black hair, secured in pigtails, swished across her shoulders as she scampered down the steps. Laughter filled her big blue eyes and colored her cheeks. Cassandra followed a few paces behind, and the joy radiating from them both lightened Stephanie's mood.

That woman had been such a gift.

She got out of her car and lowered to Maddy's level, arms extended. "There's my girl."

"Mama." Her little one barreled into her with such force, hugging her with all her thirty pounds, she nearly knocked Stephanie over.

Inhaling her daughter's bubble-gum-scented shampoo, Stephanie gave herself a firm mental nod. She could do this. She *had* to stand on her feet. If not working at the clinic, then somewhere else. She'd overcome too much to give up now.

"Seems someone sure is happy to see her mama." Cassandra patted Maddy's head. "But don't let her hightailing it out of the house fool you. She and I had ourselves loads of fun today, didn't we, pumpkin?"

Maddy's grin widened. "We found flutterbies, red wadies and happing gwassers."

Stephanie angled her head. "Butterflies I understand, but the rest?"

Cassandra laughed. "Ladybugs and grasshoppers, all of which she needed to name, of course."

"But of course." She tapped her daughter's nose and stood. "Were you good for Ms. Cassandra?"

Maddy's brow furrowed as if she had to contemplate that.

"As sweet as a buttercup." Cassandra smiled.

Maddy's signature grin returned, indicating she was relieved. "Come see what I made." She tugged Stephanie onto the porch where she'd left a handful of colorful chalk, coloring pages, drawn-on printer paper and some old blocks like one might find in antiques stores.

Stephanie picked up a picture of what appeared to be the Herron orchard. "Did you make this?"

Maddy's grin widened, and she bobbed her head. "For you."

"I love it."

"You two settle in," Cassandra said. "I'll grab us a snack. With it being peach season and all, Vincent won't be ready to eat for at least another hour yet. Hope that won't mess with your schedule."

"I'm just grateful to be here." She couldn't express how much. This place gave her hope, something she planned to hold tight to, despite her experience at the clinic.

Cassandra offered a warm smile. "We're glad that you are. This house gets way too quiet." With a wink, she disappeared into the house.

Stephanie sat cross-legged beside Maddy. "Tell me about this one." She pointed to a page nearly covered in pink and blue.

"It's a wainbow. For the fwidge so you can see it and feel happy when you eat bweakfast."

She continued turning pages faster than Stephanie's eyes could focus, then stopped on a picture of a family—mother, father and two children—gathered around a picnic table. "You like this one bestest?"

Stephanie's eyes pricked. There'd been a time when she thought she'd actually be living that dream. "It's beautiful, sweetie."

When her ex first proposed, she'd believed all his promises. Everything changed when he went to Afghanistan and, while over there, got hooked on drugs.

Thankfully, those days were behind her.

Cassandra returned and soon led them all in an "And then what happened?" game where they each added a line or two to the tale Cassandra initiated. This held Maddy's attention for a good twenty minutes before she was distracted by a ladybug crawling down one of the planks.

Stephanie and Cassandra talked some—about her field of coneflowers, how she turned their roots into echinacea tincture and all the health benefits of the herb. "We've been trying to dip our toes into the naturopathic market for some time." This led to a discussion on the history of their orchard and the challenges they faced going organic.

Cassandra had just excused herself to start supper when a black pickup approached along the dirt road dissecting the Herrons' peach groves.

Dr. Stoughton?

Stephanie stiffened, a familiar uneasiness settling into her midsection. Had he changed his mind about keeping her on? He'd said he wanted to find Dr. Wallow's program notes to chart something of a path. What if, in his reading, he'd found a loophole in her contract?

Surely he wasn't that unscrupulous. Chin up, she braced herself for whatever he'd come to say.

He stepped out of his vehicle, having traded his green work scrubs and sneakers for jeans, boots and a V-neck T-shirt. "Ma'am." Climbing the steps, he tipped his gray cowboy hat. His gaze flickered to Maddy, and a slight smile lit his eyes. "Who's this cutie?"

"That's my daughter, Maddy. She'll turn four this summer."

"Wow, such a big girl." He winked at her. "Bet you're quite a helper to Ms. Cassandra."

She nodded. "I help with the dishes and cookies and keep her house pwetty with fwowers."

Stephanie nodded. "She's Ms. Cassandra's official taste-tester for every item baked and keeps the dinner table decorated with the most beautiful dandelions."

He chuckled, but then his features sobered. "Uh, you got a minute?"

She swallowed. "Of course." She placed a hand on Maddy's shoulders. "You go color me a pretty picture while Dr. Stoughton and I talk, okay?"

Maddy studied the vet for a moment, then nodded and scooted away on her hands and knees.

Stephanie motioned to the white rocker beside one of four teal pots filled with tulips and sweet-smelling alyssum. "Can I get you some lemonade?"

"No, ma'am. Thank you." He sat.

She did as well, waiting for him to initiate the conversation she simultaneously wanted to avoid and get over with as soon as possible.

He surveyed the paper, markers, crayons and chalk scattered across the porch. "Looks like someone's been busy."

His attempts at small talk didn't ease her anxiety any.

She gave a slight smile. "She tends to go all in on whatever she's doing."

"I imagine she finds plenty on the orchard to keep her entertained."

"She enjoys it here." Stephanie loved watching Maddy run across the Herrons' yard, pick wildflowers and fill her pockets with various "treasures"—most often, pebbles.

"I bet."

An awkward silence stretched between them.

Dr. Stoughton cleared his throat. "Listen, here's the deal." He rubbed his knuckles. "I know you didn't drive halfway across the country merely to earn minimum wage."

She nodded. She came because, as unimpressive as her résumé was, she needed the experience. Plus, there was only so much a person could learn in a classroom, especially when it came to working in a rural environment where vets and their techs often had to improvise with what they had.

"You're probably aware Dr. Wallow took his internship programs seriously. He loved investing in aspiring vets and vet techs. I imagine you're expecting to receive an education able to compensate for the low salary." Sorrow filled his eyes. "And I imagine it cost you a chunk of change to get here."

"Yes, sir." It'd taken all the courage she could muster to pack up her things, get in her car, and travel over 1,300 miles from her support system. But the drive had also been invigorating. The beginning of a fresh start, for her and her daughter.

He watched Maddy for a moment as she chattered to herself about something, then shifted his attention back to Stephanie. "I'll do my best to help you get the education and hands-on experience you came for. But you need to understand the clinic has received quite a blow." Moisture pooled in his eyes. Rubbing the back of his neck, he looked away.

"I understand."

"Did you and Doc Wallow discuss anything by way of a syllabus? Any books he wanted you to read or seminars to attend?"

"Unfortunately, no. We were going to talk about all that once I arrived. So he could tailor my experience to my 'unique passions and needs.' But I'm eager to learn however I can."

And hopefully get offered full-time employment once her internship ended. But regardless of how things turned out, her time here would give her something other than waitressing to put on her résumé.

"I'll be honest with you. I don't have experience training interns, nor do I have much time to plan curriculum." He scratched his jaw. "But maybe we can come up with some sort of a game plan together—one that feels manageable to me and beneficial for you. And obviously, you can shadow me. Ask me questions and maybe try your hand at some things."

"That'd be great. Thank you, Dr. Stoughton." She appreciated him giving her the opportunity, especially considering the loss of his partner. But what if he ended up being so busy running the clinic she didn't learn much of anything?

Then her time here would be wasted.

"Please, call me Caden." His eyes softened, revealing a compassion that caused her heart to stutter. "I'm heading out to a few ranches first thing in the morning. You're welcome to come. In the meantime, how about we talk about skills, competencies and milestones to hit along the way."

She smiled. "I'd like that."

As they continued talking—about situations Caden typically faced and her personal goals—she felt the tension ease from her muscles. This conversation was going much better than she'd anticipated. Why did she always assume the worst?

She had her ex to blame for that.

Boots crunched on gravel, and she looked up. Vincent approached, wiping his forehead with a cloth, hat in hand.

Caden stood. "Sir."

"Son." He stopped at the bottom step, and his gaze swept from Stephanie to the vet and back to Stephanie again. "Everything alright?"

"Yes, sir." Caden rested a hand on his shiny belt buckle. "We were just talking about Stephanie's internship, in light of…" He took in a deep breath. "Anyone from the church call y'all yet?"

"About?"

"Can I talk with you and Ms. Cassandra for a minute?"

Vincent studied him before giving one slow nod and moving toward the house. "I imagine the missus has supper ready. We've always got room for one more."

A confusing flutter swept through Stephanie's midsection at the thought of sitting across the table from her boss. A man she needed to impress, if she wanted him to hire her full time.

Vincent held the door open. "You ladies coming?"

She nodded and urged Maddy to her feet, suddenly feeling shy and intimidated. Because Caden was so strong and handsome? And had kind and honest eyes?

She'd once thought the same about her ex-husband. She wouldn't be so foolish again.

Considering her future was on the line, it only made sense her insides would feel like jelly. But this was a first step, and so long as she kept moving forward, she and Maddy would be just fine.

Stephanie would make sure of it.

Standing in the Herrons' bright living room, Caden removed his hat and held it to his chest. The space hadn't changed much since he'd last been here, some ten years ago. The walls were still a light blue, and they'd kept their floral furniture. Same simple yet solid wooden coffee table, on which sat the same worn leather Bible and the latest cooking magazine.

The intricately carved grandfather clock Vincent's uncle gave him still stood in the corner, flanked on one side by a wooden cross and the other by the Herrons' slightly yellowed wedding photo. The long double windows facing the drive made the lamps in the centers of the handcrafted end tables unnecessary.

Only this time, a handful of toys lay scattered across the sun-faded area rug and wooden floor. Stephanie's daughter ran over to a tall pink dollhouse to the right of the stairs. She started jabbering, her voice oddly cheerful in light of what he'd come to say.

"Cassandra." Vincent sat on the shoe bench near the door to shuck off his boots. "Vet's here."

His wife emerged from the kitchen wiping her hands on a checked hand towel, her chin-length gray hair tucked behind her ears. "Caden, dear, how good to see you." Like many of his older clients who knew him as a kid, she often opted for his first name. "You're just in time for supper. I do hope you'll join us."

"I...uh..." His gaze sprang to Stephanie, and a jolt shot through him, followed by a rush of heat to his face.

What was wrong with him? Now was not the time to go all googly-eyed over some woman, regardless of how beautiful she was. Especially considering she technically worked for him. Not to mention he came to share news of his partner's death.

The shift of thought squeezed his chest, threatening to unleash emotions he fought to suppress.

He needed to focus on saying what he'd come to say with as much compassion as possible. And without breaking down. He'd hoped each conversation would help him keep his emotions in check, but seeing others grieve only made Wallow's death more real.

"Son?" Mr. Herron, and everyone else, was watching him, waiting.

Right. The supper invite.

Caden set his hat beside Vincent's on the entryway table. "I'd be honored, ma'am. Thank you." He hung back as everyone migrated into the kitchen, then followed.

Mrs. Herron had changed the curtains, from blue-and-yellow checked to bright sunflowers. Her corner shelves had become even more filled with those little knickknacks she loved so much. A porcelain cow with big black splotches. A multicolored turtle. Green plastic sprigs shot up from a lumpy, slightly lopsided vase a child must've made.

The scents of yeasty bread and roasting beef filled the room, making his stomach rumble. He quickly coughed to cover the embarrassing sound.

Vincent sat at the head of the table while Mrs. Herron handed Stephanie a pitcher of ice.

"Fill this with water, will you, dear? And miss Maddy

Mae?" Mrs. Herron handed the little girl a canister of but-
ter. "Put this on the table for me."

The child stood taller and held out her hands. She sure
was a cutie.

He'd dated a woman with a kid once, and things had
gotten pretty serious. Enough that he was contemplating
marriage. When she ended things, he'd grieved the loss of
both relationships and worried the kid had, too. Unfortunately, there wasn't anything he could do about that. The
boy's mom had cut off contact.

"Set this out, too, will you, munchkin?" Ms. Cassandra
handed Maddy a half-full jug of milk. "Got it?"

"Yup!" Maddy lugged the container, with both arms
wrapped around it, and thunked it on the table.

Once everything had been brought over, they all filled
the remaining chairs, Maddy in a booster kitty-corner to
Stephanie.

"Did you want to sit by me?" Maddy peered up at him.

His eyebrows shot up. "Sure." He sat with a grin, his
gaze springing to Stephanie.

Color sprang to her face, and she quickly glanced away.

Mr. Herron cleared his throat. "Let's pray."

Stephanie visibly stiffened before bowing her head.
Why? Because of him, or did religion make her uncomfortable?

When Mr. Herron concluded, Maddy echoed his hearty
amen, and everyone laughed.

"This girl does a person good." Mrs. Herron smoothed
a hand over the child's head, then poked her belly, producing a giggle.

Her husband nodded. "Been a while since we had children running about."

They were known for opening their homes to single
moms in need, some with troubled pasts. From what Caden
had seen, things didn't always turn out as they'd hoped.

The local hair salon had hired the last lady they'd taken in. After her training, she'd lasted maybe two weeks. Folks said she'd been skimming from the till. She'd been fired from her next job at the Brew and Hub, apparently, for the same reasons. While Caden wasn't one to trust gossip, the whole scenario made him wonder about Stephanie.

Dr. Wallow had always been drawn to those who were down on their luck. As much as Caden had admired the man—had loved him near like a father—his partner often led with more compassion than common sense.

Had that happened here? What was Stephanie's story?

Her résumé, what little there was of it, said she was from California. Odd she'd come this far for little more than minimum wage. Then again, he'd read somewhere that a lot of city folk were moving to Texas for its cheap land and slower-paced living. It made sense a single mom might want a more relaxed lifestyle. He'd only been to the West Coast once, but he wasn't hankering to go back. The traffic alone could raise a man's blood pressure.

Stephanie glanced up, once again caught him watching her, blushed and averted her gaze.

Caden gave a nervous cough and shoved the last of his roll into his mouth.

Supper finished, Mrs. Herron started clearing the table, suggesting it was time for dessert. As he'd hoped, she'd made a pan of her famous peach cobbler with oats and brown sugar crumbles.

Mr. Herron gulped the last of his sweet tea, then leveled his gaze on Caden. "You have something you need to talk with us about?"

"Yes, sir." Caden took in a deep breath. "About Dr. Wallow." As he relayed all that had happened, a familiar ache rose within.

Silence, other than Maddy's singsongy voice as she chirped lyrics about a wiggly spider, followed.

"How's his missus doing?" Mrs. Herron asked.

"Grieving." They all were. "But she's got a lot of support. Folks from the church. Family. Her kids are staying through the funeral."

"When will that be?" Cassandra dabbed at her eye with her napkin.

"I don't believe they've decided that yet. I'll let you know once they do."

"Thank you. And I'll call the quilting club gals to see how I can help. They've probably got a meal train going. I've got plenty of flowers I can donate to the funeral, and I can lend a hand with decorations."

"I'm sure Mrs. Wallow would appreciate that." His mom could make some bouquets, as well. She and his dad had plenty of wildflowers in bloom out at their bee farm. While bouquets might seem a small thing, the possibility of bringing Wallow's wife joy helped lessen the sting of Caden's sorrow.

"And Stephanie's internship?" Mr. Herron's voice was low but direct.

"She and I talked about that."

Mr. Herron looked at Stephanie. "Everything good?"

"Yeah." Once again, pink tinged her cheeks.

Her vulnerability drew him to her in a way he had no intention of entertaining.

He had a clinic to save. Not to mention, as her boss, he had to keep his wits about him, especially since he knew so little about her.

Chapter Three

The morning of her first on-site ranch visits, Stephanie deposited her things in the break room, then followed Caden out to his truck.

He hurried to open the door for her.

"Thank you." Her gaze snagged on his, and warmth swept through her. The fact that he outmuscled her by at least eighty pounds tempered her attraction. While other women might find his build attractive, her ex-husband had proven just how dangerous a man's strength could be.

He must've noticed her hesitation because his smile vanished. He closed her door, rounded the vehicle and slid into the driver's seat.

He shifted into Reverse. "Gonna be a hot one today."

She nodded, her anxiety increasing as they drove farther from the clinic.

Why did men still make her so apprehensive? She'd left John over three years ago. But she knew healing took time. Besides, her being here had to count for something.

"How long you been in Sage Creek?" Caden turned onto a winding road.

"A couple of days."

"You jumped right in, huh?"

"I guess." She'd learned of the opportunity late and then

had to secure housing. Although if she'd had any more time to think, she might've chickened out.

"Why'd you choose a vet tech degree?"

"I've always loved animals. What you see is what you get. If you're nice to them, they're nice to you."

"True." Caden offered a boyish grin that would've captivated her, had she not learned how deceptive charm could be. And how quickly a man could change. "I've got two dogs, and whenever I come home, even from a run to the store, they act like they haven't seen me in years. Well, one of them does. The other's too old for bouncing all about."

She laughed.

"Our first stop is pro bono," he said. "Not sure what that will look like going forward, but today we'll do what we can." They continued past long stretches of pasture dotted with the occasional farmhouse. "You originally from Southern California?"

"Ohio."

"This a career change for you?"

"More like something I've always wanted to pursue. I just took a while to get here."

Although his tone sounded friendly, she couldn't help feeling interrogated. Then again, this whole internship was basically a long job interview.

He turned into a ranch and continued past lush pasture areas separated by wooden fences and a steeply pitched, single-story farmhouse.

At the stables, he parked beside a four-wheeler. "These folks keep their boarders and lesson horses near the house. They temporarily quarantine new arrivals here to protect the rest of the herd from potential diseases."

He got out and grabbed two duffel-like bags from his truck bed, giving her more background information on the facility as they proceeded to the stalls. The smell of hay and horse and the occasional nicker met them as they entered the dimly lit interior.

Dr. Stoughton headed toward female voices coming from the far side of the stable.

In the last stall, a woman and child maybe ten years old, both with brown wavy hair secured in messy buns, were spreading fresh hay. The girl talked twice as fast as Maddy, if that were possible—something about trick riding, from the sounds of it.

The woman glanced up. "Hey, Doc, good to see you."

"Ma'am." He tipped his hat.

She set her rake against the wall and approached. "Dr. Wallow was a great man." Sadness filled her eyes. "Sorry for your loss."

"Thanks." He deposited his vet bag near his feet. "This is Rheanna Brewster and her daughter Amelia." He introduced Stephanie, then launched into the conversation she'd heard numerous times the day before. "Until I can hire another vet, I'll need to make adjustments."

Rheanna frowned. "What's that mean for us?"

"I'm not sure. I realize Doc Wallow spent a lot of volunteer hours out here, hours I know y'all need in order to keep this place running. How many rescues you got now?"

"Four that should be adopted out by month's end, and three I'll have a tough time rehoming. One has chronic issues and the other two might never overcome their fear of people." She slipped a hand into her pocket. "Two others came in a couple weeks ago. Wallow performed an intake exam on both of them."

Assuming other ranches were similar, Dr. Stoughton would need all the help he could get. Surely he'd hire Stephanie on permanently, so long as she worked hard, learned fast and didn't make any major mistakes. It'd beat training someone new. Right?

She glanced up to find him watching her, and a flutter

swept through her—an unwelcome response she quickly tamped down.

The last man to capture her attention had nearly broken her.

Caden spent the rest of the morning examining horses, checking growth rates and adjusting rations. Stephanie asked a question or offered a hand periodically but mostly remained quiet. She seemed especially drawn to one particularly skittish foal that lingered near the stall.

"You ready to take the lead on that one?" He motioned toward the filly.

Eyes wide, she looked to Rheanna.

"Go for it." Rheanna smiled. "Y'all are doing me a favor just coming out here. And this is a great place to learn."

"Do you have much of a medical history on her?" Stephanie asked.

Rheanna shook her head. "We took her and her mama in just over a month ago. Unfortunately, the mare went into organ failure. But this girl's a fighter." She continued with background information, including the horse's initial body condition score.

Caden's phone dinged a text, and he glanced at the screen. It was from Jeff Hollister's mom. The teen had been volunteering at the clinic for two years and had developed a deep bond with all the staff, but especially Doc Wallow. Thanks for encouraging Jeff to take time off volunteering in order to grieve. We loved Dr. Wallow dearly. He'll be greatly missed.

That he would.

Caden's eyes stung with the threat of tears. If only he'd had a few more days with Wallow. One more afternoon sitting on his porch, talking about nearly everything and nothing. Time for that fishing trip they always talked about but never took.

He turned to Stephanie with a deep, forceful breath. "What would you rate her now?"

She approached the foal slowly, almost timidly at first. Caden thought maybe her inexperience and the pressure of being watched had stalled her. But then she started talking soft and low, beckoning the filly closer.

As the foal responded, Stephanie remained still, more relaxed than he'd seen her. The foal sniffed at her hand, dangling from her side.

Rheanna chuckled. "Bet she's looking for grain."

Stephanie glanced back with a radiant smile that suggested she was doing what God had created her heart to do.

The woman was dangerously beautiful.

An image flashed through his mind of her big blue eyes staring back at him the day before, when he said they might not be able to keep her on. She'd looked so…vulnerable, almost heartbroken. As if this internship meant so much more than just a career opportunity to her.

As if, in letting her go, he'd potentially crush a long-sought dream. She was probably hoping he'd eventually hire her.

But he couldn't let his empathy, or her beauty, cloud his senses.

Still, she appeared to have a way with horses. That counted for something, though he'd feel better about this arrangement if Dr. Wallow had included more information in her file. The vague notes and sparse references concerned Caden.

Two professors had attested to her character. A third came from someone connected with an organization called Next Steps. No work experience listed. Had Stephanie been a stay-at-home mom or maybe on state assistance?

Rheanna latched the stall gate. "Renée called me."

What did his ex-girlfriend want? He tensed. "Yeah?"

"Asked about reserving a plate for our fundraising dinner."

"And?"

Humor lit her eyes. "I told her I'd give her a special rate, which happened to be triple our normal charge."

He half choked, half laughed. "What'd she say?"

"That she'd get back to me, a save-face way of ending the conversation, I'm sure."

"You didn't have to do that. I know y'all need every dollar you can raise."

She shrugged. "Figure we can do without her kind."

Around here, loyalty mattered. He was grateful for that, and mindful in relation to how he needed to run the clinic, regardless of their challenges. Although loyalty hadn't stopped some of the clinic's clients from switching to that new, more "modern" practice one town over. Wallow had always said there was plenty of business for both facilities, but Caden wasn't so sure.

Doc's death could be the nudge other folks needed to make the change.

"You're coming, right?" Rheanna leaned against the wall. "Prime rib buffet, live band, line dancing. Plus, we've got some great items up for auction."

"I'd love to support y'all, but I can't swing the fifty dollars for a plate."

"We'll waive that. To thank you for all the hours of animal care we've received."

"I don't know." He rubbed the back of his neck. "I'm not really into those types of shindigs. That was more Wallow's thing."

"You don't think he went for fun, do you? He was networking."

Interesting. Caden had always assumed the man enjoyed being around people. How else had he kept the clinic running that Caden hadn't realized?

He scratched his chin. "I'll think about it."

"I'll send you an e-vite." She turned to Stephanie, who now stood beside them. "You should come, too. It'd be a great way to get to know the community."

Heat surged to his face as an image of the two of them on the dance floor rushed to mind, her big beautiful eyes locked on his.

Her accompanying him to an event that practically necessitated close contact was *not* a good idea. But Rheanna did have a point. If Caden wanted the practice to survive, he'd need to learn how to network, now more than ever. Some of their clients wouldn't be happy about losing their primary vet, especially since many of them still remembered Caden as that quiet homeschooled Stoughton kid. The family "baby" as his mama had often called him.

He'd been fighting that label ever since. Maybe now that he ran the practice, he could finally earn the respect of Sage Creek's elders.

Stephanie's soft laugh disrupted his thoughts and temporarily froze his brain.

Two and a half months, and then she'd be gone.

Unless he hired her on full time. Then he—and his heart—would be in big trouble.

He spent the rest of the afternoon fighting his wayward thoughts so that he could remain the clear-minded professional he was. Stephanie's sweet nature and shy smile didn't help his efforts any. With each visit, he saw more of her tenderness and almost innate ability to connect with animals.

Back in the truck, he waited for her to snap her seat belt into place, then shifted into gear. "Any questions from our on-site visits so far?"

She shot him what appeared to be a timid glance, then nodded. "I'd love to know more about the horse rescue. How'd they get started?"

Was she interested in doing something similar? After

how she'd responded to the horses, and how they'd responded to her, he could see that. "Rheanna, her daughter and best friend moved here when she learned she inherited the ranch two years ago. They arrived, inexperienced, to find the place in shambles."

"I've heard that can happen with nonprofits."

"It was once a thriving horse ranch." He turned onto the main road. "But it fell into decline when her uncle developed Alzheimer's. Anyway, one afternoon, Rheanna went into town to drop off flyers. Hoping to get competent help, which they needed badly. And she got roped into an emergency rescue operation—with her former high school boyfriend."

"That must've been interesting."

"Initially, yes. But things turned out well enough. They eventually married." He cast her a sideways glance. Was Maddy's dad still in the picture?

That was none of his business.

He cleared his throat. "What'd you think about the sheep farm?"

"It was interesting. I'd learned about bluetongue but had never encountered real-life examples. That was…"

"Hard to see?" With a 50 percent mortality rate, it was a nasty disease that caused the mucus membranes to swell and become hemorrhagic.

She nodded.

Whether a dog, pig, horse or ewe, animal deaths never got easier. "Thankfully, we save more than we lose."

When they returned to the clinic, Jeff Hollister, their teen volunteer, was parked in the lot, waiting in his car. Caden pulled alongside him, and the two stepped out of their vehicles simultaneously.

Caden introduced them to each other, explaining their respective roles. "Jeff helps answer the phone, walk our borders, when we've got them, clean the exam rooms between visits—basically, whatever we need."

Stephanie tucked a windblown lock of hair behind her ear. "What a blessing you must be."

"I do what I can." Jeff paused. "My mom said you called. About Doc Wallow?"

Caden nodded, his heart squeezing. "Sorry, bud."

He shrugged. "Me, too. For you, I mean. Paul's inside?"

Caden glanced first at the janitor's truck, parked on the other end of the lot, then to the clinic behind them. "Seems so."

Jeff gave one quick nod. "Guess I best get in, then." He turned to go.

Caden placed a hand on his shoulder. "We're alright. You go home. Give yourself time to grieve."

Jeff started rubbing his fist. "I want to help." His voice came out tighter than normal. Wobbly.

"I appreciate that, but we'll be okay," Caden said.

Jeff studied him a moment longer, looking like he wanted to say more, but then he told Stephanie it was nice to meet her and left.

Heart heavy, Caden watched him drive away, then walked Stephanie to her car. "Have a good night."

Her smile accentuated her beauty. "See you in the morning."

"Bright and early." Too early, if his fatigued muscles had any say in the matter. He needed to hire another vet fast. He'd place help-wanted ads on job application sites during his lunch tomorrow.

Did he really think anyone would want to come to such a small town? For a rural salary?

Caden's posting wouldn't be popular, but he had to try. In the meantime, he'd contact a vet relief company. Then he'd work on getting former clients to return.

Maybe he'd encounter a few of them at Rheanna's barn

dance. An image of Stephanie wearing a cute summer dress, her long black hair cascading over her bare, delicate shoulders came to mind, and his pulse immediately spiked.

He never should've agreed to that shindig, but he couldn't back out now. Besides, what would he say? "Sorry, but I'm worried your beauty could prove challenging"?

He scrubbed a hand over his face and entered the clinic, causing the bell to jingle.

"Doc?" Paul's voice drifted into the lobby, followed by booted footsteps. "That you?"

"Yep."

He met the clinic janitor, who stood maybe six-foot-two and weighed about a buck seventy-five, near exam room one. The grief reflected in the man's eyes was palpable, and his brown hair hung greasy and shaggy, in need of a wash.

"Hey." Paul squeezed the brim of his ball cap. "How're you doing?"

Caden gave a weak shrug. If he thought about Wallow's death too much, let himself feel the loss, he feared his grief might become a seeping, all-consuming wound.

He'd best honor his friend by making sure the clinic thrived.

He pocketed his keys. "What about you? If you need the night off…"

"Can't afford that."

Caden understood.

His cell rang. He glanced at the screen, and a lump lodged in his throat. "Can you excuse me?"

Paul nodded and shuffled toward the back storage closet where they kept their cleaning supplies.

Caden answered his phone midway through another ring. "Marla, hello." He wasn't sure what to say to Wallow's wife. What *did* a person say to a woman who'd lost her husband of forty-some years?

He expressed his condolences as best he could, then,

sensing she needed lighter conversation, shifted to small talk. Not wanting to add guilt to Marla's grief, he omitted stories of worried pet owners he and Lisa had dealt with.

"That new intern working out okay?" she asked.

As his thoughts jumped to Stephanie, his heart skipped a beat. "So far, yeah."

"Treat her kindly."

"Of course." But the way she said that concerned him. "Why? Is there something I should know?"

"No. She just…comes from a rough place is all."

He rubbed his temple. So, she was one of Wallow's charity cases. He'd need to keep an eye on her, to ensure she was competent *and* trustworthy.

"I was calling about the funeral." Marla's voice cracked. "It's this Friday at two. I know that'll cut into clinic hours."

"I'm not worried about that." He owed Wallow's family as much and more. "Your husband was a good man." His eyes burned. "Taking a chance on hiring some punk kid fresh out of college, and with a less-than-stellar GPA."

"He was always finding someone to coach up." Her tone carried a smile.

"That he was."

After ending the call, Caden grabbed his cowboy hat from the corner of his desk and headed outside for some fresh air to process. The temperature had dropped with the setting sun, and streaks of purple and pink stretched across the horizon. In the fallow grasslands bordering the pasture, bluebonnets, primrose and tiny yellow flowers danced in the evening breeze. Somewhere in the distance, a mockingbird sang.

He stood there, watching the wind-stirred grass wave, for some time, processing all that had occurred and all he still had to do. He'd long dreamed about having his own practice, but never like this.

His phone rang again. He glanced at the screen, and

his breath hitched. "Stephanie." He'd answered much too quickly. *Rein it in, buddy.* Since when had he started acting like a girl-crazy middle schooler? "Is everything okay?"

"Yes, I was just…" Her soft voice triggered images of her equally soft features and the way she rubbed at her collarbone when initiating conversation. "I talked with the Herrons about the fundraiser."

He held his breath.

"Mrs. Herron's free to watch my daughter that night."

A grin twitched on his lips. "Does that mean you can go?"

"Yes."

The grin broke loose.

The fact that he found himself smiling like a kid on the first day of baseball season demonstrated what a bad idea this was. But Rheanna was right—he needed to participate in community functions, for the clinic's sake.

He breathed deep to maintain his good sense. "Great. I'll pick you up next Saturday at six p.m."

"Okay." She paused. "What should I wear?"

That was like asking a guy what hair or makeup products a woman should buy. "Uh. Some kind of dress or something." The faint floral smell of her shampoo and the feel of her soft hand in his as they slowly danced, perfectly in step, came to mind. He quickly shook it off, chastising himself for the umpteenth time since he'd answered the call.

"Like a gown?" she asked.

"What?"

"A ball gown?"

"You thought…?" She really was a city girl, wasn't she? How would she fare with Sage Creek's simpler and quieter community? "It's not that kind of ball. More like a barn dance than anything."

"Oh." She almost sounded disappointed. "Alright."

"Need me to call around to see what the other ladies plan

on wearing?" He'd heard Lisa do that a time or two—ring up nearly every woman she knew to compare outfits for some shindig. Like getting dolled up was a social occasion.

"That's okay. But thank you."

He felt a sudden urge to prolong their conversation. "Listen, I spoke with Mrs. Wallow a bit ago." He relayed the funeral information. "You don't have to go, but I figured—"

"I'd like to. While I didn't know the doctor well, I greatly appreciate him giving me the internship opportunity."

"Okay. Want to catch a ride with me?" He told himself he was merely trying to be polite, but the anticipation building within suggested otherwise.

An awkward silence followed. "Sure. Thank you."

That meant they'd be spending nearly every day together for the next two weeks, when he needed to maintain a professional distance.

The funeral he could handle. There wasn't anything remotely romantic about that. But the barn dance?

What had he gotten himself into?

Chapter Four

The next morning, Stephanie hesitated outside the clinic, feeling jittery and shy at seeing Caden again. Because he'd invited her to the barn dance? Although Rheanna had done that, for purely business reasons.

Still, a dance. Did Caden need her help with networking? What if she bumbled her words? Plus, she had nothing to wear other than scrubs and faded blue jeans.

She was being ridiculous. This wasn't some formal, fancy presentation, and she was an adult. Besides, Caden would probably do most of the talking.

She couldn't remember the last time she'd attended a dance.

Actually, she could—senior prom. With John. He'd seemed so adoring. She'd misread his possessiveness for attention. Maybe, if not for his tour in Afghanistan and subsequent drug use, everything would've been fine.

Once he'd returned, his jealousy and temper had intensified.

Lisa barged toward her, jolting Stephanie's thoughts back to the present. She flung the door open. "You going to stand there all day?"

Stephanie glanced past her to find Caden watching. His

warm smile, and the fact that she probably looked like an idiot standing at the door so long, made her blush.

"Sorry." She hurried inside and followed Lisa to the reception desk.

"Need to keep your wits about you." Lisa frowned. "This isn't the time or place for mental vacations. We've got a cat coming in for a suspected lung infection. A few wellness exams, an itchy guinea pig, and a golden retriever who's refusing to eat and started vomiting last night. Most likely he swallowed something. He'll probably need an X-ray. And that's all before noon."

Stephanie nodded. She was relatively experienced with domesticated animals. Maybe today would allow her to display her competence.

Caden came to her side holding a stack of files under his arm. "Morning. I printed off some vet tech job descriptions and thought we could use the competencies as curriculum guides." He glanced at his phone screen. "I know we don't have a lot of time before the day turns crazy, but let's pop into my office to see if we can't develop something of a road map."

Stephanie smiled. "I greatly appreciate this."

He gave a slight grin. "That's why you joined that Next Steps program in California?"

She nodded and followed him down the hall to his office. As she stepped into the room, the musky scent of his aftershave and the enclosed environment stirred conflicting emotions within her. Her attraction to him scared her.

"You okay?"

She took a deep breath, relaxing her tense muscles on the exhale. "Of course." She sat in the chair across the desk from him.

He opened a three-ring binder and turned it so she could see the documents inside. "I got these from various job search websites. They're all pretty similar."

She liked the reminder that people were indeed looking for vet techs.

"When hired, you'll be expected to perform routine exams, follow up on patients after treatments." He read through the bulleted list on the first paper. "Have you drawn blood before?"

"Some."

"How comfortable are you with the procedure?"

She gave a nervous laugh. "I'm sure I could use more practice."

"We'll make sure that happens, then."

This led to a discussion on her proficiencies and weaknesses and how he could provide her with growth opportunities. His eyes lit up as they talked. It was obvious he loved what he did and that he truly wanted to teach her. As if he cared about her future.

Her dreams and ambitions had always seemed to threaten John.

Eventually, she'd quit dreaming. But now? It was like she was rediscovering herself, a process she found equally invigorating and terrifying.

She glanced at a photo on Caden's desk. In it, he sat on a boulder with a fluffy white dog on his lap and a black Lab mix seated by his feet. Caden wore a blue windbreaker, shorts, hiking boots and a wide grin.

He must've followed her line of sight, because he picked up the frame. "This is Bella and Rocky. Both were rescues, this little guy after a procedure I can only assume his owner couldn't pay. Bella was likely a breeding dog. Found her outside my clinic one morning. Someone—her owner, a concerned neighbor, who knows—must've dropped her off." He shook his head. "She sure was in a bad state. Thin, frightened, nails so long they'd begun to curl under."

"You get that a lot?"

"It happens. Usually it's not hard to find new owners.

You'll discover Sage Creek folks have big hearts, which I'm super thankful for. Obviously, I can't take in every furry critter that meanders by. But with Bella, I didn't even try. I just had a gut feeling she belonged to me."

"She's beautiful."

"Thanks." He eyed the picture a moment longer, as if remembering the day it was taken, then returned it to his desk. He tapped his documents. "I would love for you to feel proficient in each of these responsibilities before your internship concludes. Using that as a guide, I developed something of a timeline. Figured you could begin by shadowing me with me steadily increasing your responsibilities." He turned the page. "Does this look reasonable?"

Two months. To master the skills, yes, but even more so to prove her competence. "This looks great, and I really appreciate you taking the time to outline this all for me."

"Of course." He tapped his phone screen and stood. "We can talk more about this later. As far as today goes…" He released a breath and raked a hand through his hair. "I'm not sure how much direct training I'll be able to do."

"I understand."

"Actually, I could really use your help with something."

"Absolutely."

Lisa poked her head into the office. "Doc? Your first appointment is here."

He stood with a nod, then faced Stephanie. "I'm going to be placing an order soon, and there appears to be problems with our inventory numbers. I'd like for you to get me an accurate count. Please also check our medication expiration dates, for cleanliness, that sort of thing."

"Absolutely." She hoped her smile hid her nervousness. She'd passed all her lab work in college, but not without significant effort.

"I can take care of that," Lisa said.

He shook his head. "This will serve as a pharmacology

review for her, as eventually she'll be helping with calculations and compounding. Plus, I really need you out front to field questions and reassure patients. I imagine we'll hear from numerous concerned clients today. They'll need to see a familiar face, hear a familiar voice."

Lisa released a huff. "Whatever." She strode off.

Did she find Stephanie incapable? Worry that she would try to steal her job?

Some clinics' techs did a lot of reception work as well, and Caden's funds were clearly limited. Maybe Lisa feared that, unable to pay both positions, he'd choose the person with more education.

No matter how financially desperate, Stephanie wasn't the job-stealing type.

Caden handed Stephanie a clipboard and pencil, then led the way to the lobby. They'd just reached the desk when a tall, lanky man with slightly sunken cheeks walked in with a German shepherd-Lab mix tugging on his leash.

"Well, look who's here." Caden's tone matched his smile.

The dog's animation increased. Panting and straining, he wagged his tail with such enthusiasm, the back half of his body swayed.

"Cookie, my man." Caden rounded the desk to scratch behind the dog's ears. "I'm excited to see you, too, buddy." He shook hands with the owner. "Wish all my patients were this enthusiastic."

The man laughed. "I'm not sure he'd be so excited if he knew why we're here." He had curly black hair and a thin goatee and a paint-splotched T-shirt and jeans cut into shorts.

"Nothing but a pinprick, isn't that right, boy?" Caden started to head to the nearest exam room but halted when the front door chimed open.

Stephanie followed his line of sight to a hunchbacked older woman who entered with a Chihuahua, nearly swallowed by a ruffled pink blanket. A floppy bow sat cockeyed on the dog's head. The woman wore a flowing purple-and-green overdress-type outfit with large teardrop-shaped earrings and a matching chunky necklace.

One of them smelled like a strange mixture of lemon and garlic.

Caden inched back to the desk and eyed the computer screen.

Lisa shook her head. "She doesn't have an appointment."

He nodded, then faced the client. "Have a seat, ma'am. I'll be with you soon."

Her face puckered, her maroon lipstick bleeding into the wrinkles fanning from her mouth. "I don't have much time, and like I explained to your receptionist over the phone, LouLou has a bellyache." She scrunched her puffy silver hair.

"I understand, and I promise not to keep you waiting more—"

"Stephanie could get her started." Lisa flicked Stephanie's arm. "Ain't that right?" She leaned closer and cupped a hand over her mouth. "It'll be good training."

"Uh, sure." Honestly, she'd much rather spend her time with the animals, so long as Caden wasn't in too much of a hurry to place his order. She could always work on the inventory during slow periods.

Assuming there were slow periods.

Facing the woman, she offered her most professional smile. "Ma'am."

The woman's lips remained pursed.

Something told Stephanie this interaction wouldn't be pleasant, and her first real patient no less. But Lisa was right. LouLou's owner could give Stephanie practice with more challenging clients.

This situation might even allow her to demonstrate people skills.

For future employment. That was the only reason she wanted to impress Caden.

Not because her insides somersaulted whenever his hazel eyes shifted her way.

Caden studied her, as if uncertain. "Alright. Lisa, can you give Ms....?"

"Mason." The woman sounded like she'd just bitten a rotten pickle.

"Give Ms. Mason a new patient form to fill out, and Stephanie, can you take our friends to exam room three?"

She tried to remember which one that was. She must've looked as confused as she felt because Lisa stood. "Come on." She grabbed a clipboard with a sheet of paper and pen on it. "I'll show you."

"Oh, great." Ms. Mason rolled her eyes. "We get stuck with the rookie."

Caden appeared to second-guess allowing Stephanie to begin the appointment.

She flashed what she hoped resembled a confident smile, then rotated toward the woman. "Don't worry. While new to this clinic, I'm comfortable in an exam room. And Dr. Stoughton will join us soon."

Ms. Mason followed, mumbling, into the small, gray-walled and linoleum-floored space. The vents above circulated the aroma of antiseptic with a hint of pine-scented cleaner.

"LouLou is it?" Stephanie motioned to an empty chair against the wall.

Ms. Mason nodded. Sitting, she clutched her pooch on her lap as if afraid Stephanie might try to snatch it.

Stephanie remained standing. "How long have you had her?"

"Since she was a pup."

"And that's been...?"

"Going on fifteen years." The woman pumped her foot.

"Has she traveled outside of the area recently?"

"No, but we did just move here. I know that upset her."

"That's understandable." A move could easily exacerbate the Chihuahua's naturally anxious disposition. If the dog was as high-strung as this woman seemed, the two could easily play off each other, resulting in upset bellies for them both.

Maybe small talk would help put the woman at ease. "Where are you from?"

"I don't see how that's your business."

Stephanie's eyebrows shot up, but she quickly covered with a polite smile. "How's her appetite?"

"Like I said, she's got a stomachache." She huffed. "I'm the one that should be asking you and that teenybopper vet all the questions."

Teenybopper? Clearly this was going to take a while.

Doing her best to keep her expression smooth and pleasant, Stephanie pulled the rolling stool over. "Dr. Stoughton might be the best person for this, but I'll answer what I can."

"Ah. So, you're not as knowledgeable as you pretend, huh?"

"What I mean is—"

"How many veterinarians work at this practice?"

"One."

"That kid out there is all you've got?"

"Currently, yes."

"So, y'all are planning on hiring on more staff?"

She hoped so, at least as far as she was concerned. But as to whether or not Dr. Stoughton would find a new partner? "You'll have to discuss that with the doctor."

"What were all those folders stacked on that desk out there?" She jerked a thumb toward the exam door.

Why would she ask such an odd question? "Medical files."

"Y'all seem disorganized to me. How do I know the care LouLou receives will be any better?"

"I can assure you, Dr. Stoughton is very capable and conscientious." At least, that was her assumption. But she hadn't known him long. Caden certainly seemed frazzled. For good reason, but still.

The woman kept firing questions faster than Stephanie could process, getting her dog worked up, as well. "What's your title?"

"I graduated with a vet tech degree."

"Here. What's your role here?"

"To assist Dr. Stoughton as he—"

"Why are you avoiding my question? You got something to hide?" The woman sprang to her feet, causing her dog to yap louder.

"No, ma'am. Dr. Wallow—"

"Who's Dr. Wallow?"

"He was Dr. Stoughton's partner."

"Was?"

Oh, boy. "Yes, but unfortunately, he passed away rather suddenly."

A look of compassion momentarily softened the woman's expression. But then she narrowed her eyes onto Stephanie with the same level of scrutiny one might expect during a criminal investigation. Then again, that's what the entire interchange had felt like from the get-go. Rather than allay the woman's concerns, as Stephanie had hoped to do, her answers had only increased her distrust and irritation.

Things elevated considerably once Lisa escorted the woman's husband in. At about six foot three and maybe three hundred pounds, the man's scowling demeanor made his wife's seem almost pleasant in comparison. His wavy hair that reached just below his chin and his bushy eyebrows made him look all the more menacing.

Almost immediately, he joined in his wife's barrage,

his deep, booming voice overpowering hers and the dog's now-frantic yapping.

An image flashed through Stephanie's mind of her ex-husband towering over her, face red and veins bulging on his neck, hand raised and ready to strike.

Her throat felt like it was closing, and she struggled to get enough air. Dizziness swept over her, churning her stomach. Her body practically caved inward, and she inched backward until the counter's edge dug into her back.

In her peripheral vision, she saw Caden enter. Heard his voice and sensed the others had quieted—though the dog's barking had escalated.

"Sorry to keep you waiting." Caden looked from Stephanie to the owners. "Is everything alright?"

She struggled to form her thoughts into both professional and informative words.

"Forget this." The man huffed. "Come on, Sharon. We can do better for LouLou. Let's go check out that traveling vet we saw flyers for."

Sharon stood, clutching her yelping dog to her chest, and followed her husband out, both of them muttering and complaining.

Caden trailed them into the hall, speaking professional apologies.

He returned a moment later. "What happened?"

Tears coursed down Stephanie's cheeks despite her efforts to hold them in. "I'm sorry." She did her best to explain, wishing she'd handled the situation better. Had handled herself better.

Instead, she'd frozen.

What if Caden decided she couldn't do this job?

Caden's heart lurched watching Stephanie look so broken, so fragile. He hurried to her side as she lost her battle against another wave of tears. He placed an arm around her shoulder, wanting to protect her. She tensed and seemed to tremble slightly.

Whatever those people had said had really shaken her up.

He dropped his arm, and she inched away from him.

"It's okay," he said. "That couple came in looking for a fight. I doubt you could've said anything to make them happy."

Was that true? Granted, those clients had been challenging, to put it mildly. But they weren't the worst this clinic had dealt with, or would in the future. Did Stephanie have the grit and interpersonal skills to manage their high-maintenance pet owners?

Once again, he wondered why Dr. Wallow had offered her this position, why the Herrons had opened their home to her.

What was her story?

Stephanie palmed away her tears, sniffed and straightened. "I apologize for my reaction. It won't happen again."

He felt a strong urge to comfort her, which of course wouldn't be appropriate. Clearing his throat, he added professional distance between them. "Do you need a moment?"

"I'm okay." She offered that shy smile that always turned his insides to mush.

That smile, coupled with her tears, could get him and this office into serious trouble, if he wasn't careful.

"Would you like me to work on the medications now?"

He studied her for a moment, then nodded. "Sure. Do what you can today, and I'll make sure you have time to finish tomorrow."

He walked her to where they stored their medicine, gave her a quick rundown of where they kept what, then hurried back to the reception area.

The phone rang. Lisa was talking with a client, so Caden answered. "Well, hello, Mrs. Starnes. How's Benji doing?"

"Fine, but he's short a few pain pills."

He frowned. "Are you certain?"

"I'm extremely careful, Doctor."

"Yes, of course."

"I count and document everything my baby puts in his mouth, especially medications. I was putting them in his pill holder and came up short."

He'd read articles about drug addicts targeting clinics in bigger cities, but he couldn't imagine sweet Mrs. Starnes doing that. "I know you're quite meticulous in your care. Did you want to—"

"We'll be fine. I doubt Benji will need all the pain medication anyway. I just wanted you to know."

"I appreciate that. Thank you." He replaced the phone in its cradle.

"What was that about?" Lisa asked.

He relayed the conversation.

She nodded. "Poor lady is getting up there. Dementia runs in her family, you know."

"I haven't noticed anything concerning in her behavior."

"Yeah, well, we examine pets, not the owners, right? Just something to keep an eye on."

As if he didn't have enough to manage. But Lisa was right. He couldn't have pet owners misplacing medication.

Or interns coming apart in front of clients, even those as prickly as LouLou's owners.

Especially with Wallow gone. The clinic needed to convey competence, not panic. And if Stephanie had a similar reaction in the near future?

He'd deal with that when, if, the time came.

Chapter Five

The cupboards and locked storage compartment were a mess, but at least many of the medications were up-to-date.

Stephanie had just made it to the diazepam when Lisa poked her head in. "Come help with our last few patients so I can handle some things with less interruptions. If Doc gives you slack, tell him I'll help you in here when I get a chance. Though not today, of course, with the funeral and all."

Stephanie didn't want to challenge a senior coworker. But did Lisa have the authority to override Caden's request? Hopefully, if he got upset, it'd be with Lisa, not her.

"Okay." Stephanie followed her back to the reception area.

"You coming to the funeral?"

"Yeah, but..." She couldn't *not* go, but she also couldn't show up in scrubs or jeans. "I don't have anything black to wear." Or the funds for shopping.

"How about you cut out early and head over to My Sister's Resale?" Lisa tossed a crumpled sticky note into the trash. "My friend owns the place. She'll help you find something. So long as it's black, it'll do."

"I...uh..." How ridiculous would it sound to say she couldn't even afford a secondhand shirt?

Just then, Caden appeared at her side. His musky cologne merged with the sharper scent of hand sanitizer. "Is everything alright?"

Heat seeped into her face, likely giving her a blotchy red complexion. "Yes, of course." If only she could avoid this conversation, but pretending she wasn't poor wouldn't help. She took in a deep breath and relayed her dilemma. "I don't want to appear disrespectful—in how I dress or in not attending."

He surveyed the lobby. "After our last appointment today, I'll take you into town to buy something. Consider it a work expense, which of course, it is."

"You don't have to do that."

He offered a gentle smile. "I do, for Dr. Wallow and his family."

And for that same reason, she'd accept his offer, as hard as that was. But every ounce of charity only fueled her determination. She *would* find steady employment—a career. Then she'd show others the same generosity she'd received.

"Do you have anything for the fundraising dance?"

Stephanie dropped her gaze. Although Lisa didn't say anything, she could sense the woman watching her. And while she knew she was probably misreading things due to her own insecurities, she couldn't help but feel judged.

"Might as well find something for that, as well."

Why was he being so nice? And what kind of strings might he attach to his generosity? "I'll pay you back."

He stopped flipping through pages on a clipboard and shook his head. "Like I said, this is a work expense, the dance especially." The set of his jaw suggested she'd be rude to argue. Besides, she was probably overthinking. Like her therapist used to say, some people are simply kind.

Her ex-husband had made her lose sight of that. It was time she regained perspective.

The phone rang, and Lisa answered. Listening, she nodded periodically. "These things happen." She ended the call. "That was our last appointment. Owner said Ralphie took off running when she tried to get him into the van. She chased after him, but that only sent him into the woods."

"Well, then…" He faced Stephanie. "You ready?"

Her stomach gave an odd flip with equal parts anticipation and apprehension like it did whenever she was about to get into his truck with him.

Thankfully, as they drove to town, he immediately engaged her in a casual conversation.

"Sage Creek obviously won't have any of those fancy department stores like in California, but I'm sure we'll find something."

"I adore your downtown area."

"Got to admit, I'm partial to it. Mostly because of the people. Can't go far around here without running into a friend." Railroad crossing lights flashed up ahead. "How're you liking things out at the Herrons'?"

"They've been amazing." While his question appeared harmless enough, she worried where it might lead. She had no desire to discuss her past or anything related to it. "Cassandra said you and your brothers used to help with the peach festival each year?"

"I worked out there every summer through high school and halfway through my undergrad. They paid great, and it was fun."

"I imagine she kept you well fed. She made four peach pies and three cobblers for today's memorial service."

He laughed. "She always was quick with her desserts. You like to bake?"

An ache filled her heart. "I used to. With my grandmother."

"She still around?"

"Yeah. She lives in a retirement home on the West Coast."

"Where you're from?"

She tensed as the conversation drifted dangerously close to her past. "She's in Washington. What about you? Do you have family in town?"

"Three generations. My parents own a bee farm ten miles east. My granddaddy lives an afternoon's gallop away. Most of my siblings stayed close. One farms. Another teaches and coaches—basketball—at Sage Creek High." He soon launched into tales of family adventures like making fishing rods from salvaged twine and rope swings over the crick.

"Until the branch snapped and my brother fractured his arm." He tipped his hat to an oncoming driver. "'Course, that didn't bother him much. He was more upset that our brilliant contraption broke. But Mama banned us from that tree after that. Teased that she didn't have money to waste on emergency room visits. What about your folks?"

"My mom works retail in Ohio."

"How'd you end up in California?"

"I've asked myself that same question."

Luckily, they reached the boutique before he could press her further. She jumped out of the truck the moment he parked and waited for him on the curb.

The scent of sweet alyssum drifted from one of the many flowerpots dangling from hooks on old-style lampposts. Simple wooden signs hung above the brick storefronts stretching down the street in both directions, and chirping birds merged with the distant sound of music coming from a local business.

Her phone rang. She glanced at the screen and smiled. It was her mom.

She politely excused herself to answer. "Hey, Mom."

"Hi. You okay?" Her tone sounded tight.

"I'm fine. Why?"

"John was paroled."

Stephanie's breath caught, and the ground beneath her seemed to sway. "Okay." *He has no idea where I am. He can't find us. We're safe here.*

Her mental pep talk wasn't helping. "Has he contacted you?"

"I kept my new number and address unlisted, remember?"

"Right. Good. That's good." They were both safe.

"I didn't want to frighten you. I just felt you should know."

"I appreciate that."

"Love you, and give Maddy-girl a hug from Grandma."

"I will." Call ended, Stephanie returned her phone to her purse and rejoined Caden, determined not to obsess over an unlikely what-if scenario.

"Well, I'll be."

They spun around to see three older women walking toward them with amused expressions.

"I don't believe we've had the privilege of meeting." The shortest of the three, Karen, a woman with deep wrinkles and kind, laughing eyes, gave a mischievous smile.

Caden made introductions.

Margie, the plump woman in the middle, made an exaggerated point to glance up and down the sidewalk. "I don't see a lot of critters around here needing vet care. Do you, Lucy?"

Caden quickly explained the reason for his and Stephanie's downtown visit.

"Oh, we can help with that." Margie's eyes twinkled. "Can't we, girls?" She looped an arm through Stephanie's and the three ladies whisked her into the boutique.

Lost for words, she glanced behind her to see Caden following, chuckling.

"Don't dally, now." The ladies tugged her toward a back clearance rack.

"Let me guess." Lucy pulled out a crew-neck dress with long, lace-adorned sleeves and held it in front of Stephanie. "Size six?"

Before she could answer, Margie plopped a large floppy hat on her head. "Isn't this darling? It'll shield your eyes from the sun."

"Indeed." Lucy gave a quick, firm nod, then handed Stephanie a button-up blouse and pair of slacks. "How about you try these on." She ushered Stephanie into a small dressing room with a velvet curtain for a door.

The way the ladies fussed over her reminded her of when her mom took her shopping for her prom dress. Although they had little money to spare, her mom had insisted on buying Stephanie "something fabulous." They'd landed on an elegant wine-colored gown layered with light fabric. While Stephanie had been grateful for the gift, she'd cherished the time spent with her mom most.

How she missed her.

"Where you from, sugar?" Margie asked from the other side.

Stephanie hesitated. "Southern California."

One of the ladies whistled.

"You're sure a long way from home," Lucy said. "Bet this feels like a bit of a culture shock."

Margie laughed. "In a good way, am I right?"

"Yes, ma'am." They had no idea how much. To not have to worry about her ex-husband hunting her down. Well, to worry about that less.

She stepped out wearing the dress, and her gaze immediately shot to Caden. The surprised admiration in his eyes sent a flutter through her.

Blushing, she quickly focused on the ladies gathered in front of her. "Everyone has been so lovely and welcoming."

"Where are you staying?" Clearly Margie had no shortage of questions or any hesitation in asking.

When she told them, they grew quiet. Margie's eyebrows shot up, and she and Lucy exchanged an odd look.

They acted as if her housing situation labeled her somehow, and not in a good way.

Was that why Lisa seemed so leery of her and why Caden had been so reluctant to keep her on? If so, would whatever negative associations people formed hinder her future employment—not just with Caden but anywhere in Sage Creek?

Whatever they were thinking, she'd simply have to prove them wrong.

Thirty minutes later, Stephanie left the boutique in funeral attire—she'd changed in the dressing room—and with a V-neck, open-back, powder-blue dress with spaghetti straps, and boots they'd snagged for ten dollars.

She smiled. "Thanks again. That was fun." It truly had been, and way less awkward than if she'd shopped with Caden alone.

"Anytime." Lucy gave her a firm hug. "See you this afternoon."

With cheerful waves, the women sauntered off, and Caden and Stephanie headed the opposite direction toward his truck.

By the time they arrived at the funeral, the church parking lot and nearly all the pews were filled. Clearly Dr. Wallow had left quite a legacy. It appeared nearly all of Sage Creek had come to show their respect.

"Yoo-hoo!" Margie's high-pitched voice pierced the din.

Stephanie turned to see her waving a gloved hand. Margie pointed to an empty section of pew to her left. Her friends from the boutique sat to her right, all three of them looking at Stephanie and Caden.

"It appears your new friends saved us a seat." Hand on her elbow, he guided her around two ladies sniffling and hugging in the aisle. His calloused skin felt rough against hers, reminding her of his strength.

A strength that drew her to him and elevated her caution. Yet with every interaction, his gentleness and easy smile were overriding her anxiety, creating a new concern in its place.

She could easily fall for this man.

That would be completely impractical, him being her boss and all. But did her attraction suggest she was ready to date? Could she trust her judgment? Raised by a single mom, she hadn't a clue what a godly man acted like, a godly marriage looked like. Her grandparents had been amazing, but had divorced when she was in early elementary school.

Yet Maddy deserved a dad. A kind and loving father who'd take her fishing or hiking and was always there to cheer her on.

If Stephanie *did* remarry, she'd make certain her husband was worth holding tight to, and that he'd hold tight to her as well—in love, not control.

After the funeral, Caden approached Jeff, who'd been hanging back, standing in the shade of a Texas ash.

"Hey." The boy raised shadowed, bloodshot eyes.

"Hi, bud." Caden gave his shoulder a firm squeeze.

The boy broke down, face in his hands, torso shaking.

"It's okay." Caden pulled Jeff, the size of a man, but still very much a kid, to him. "It's okay." Tears stung his eyes, too, but he blinked them back and focused on the stream of people returning to the church for the wake.

Jeff pulled away and dried his face with his sleeve. "Sorry. I guess I just…" He shook his head and looked away.

Caden understood. Sometimes there simply weren't words. He still struggled to grasp that Wallow was really gone. "Doc loved you like a son." He worried if he said anything else, he'd break down, as well. "You need to talk, I'm here. Always."

Jeff stared at the ground, and after a few silent moments, excused himself. Caden took a deep breath and released it slowly, then merged with the last few stragglers leaving the cemetery.

Jeff's mom met him at the gate. "I'm glad he reached out to you. I'm worried about him."

"Just give him time."

"It's not just..." Her brow furrowed. "I shouldn't be bothering you with this. I apologize."

"It's no bother. I care about the boy."

Tears welled in her eyes. "I know. I appreciate it." She turned and left.

He remained where he was, his thoughts sluggish. Everything felt so raw, every conversation like a prick on an open wound.

Where was Stephanie? He felt a sense of responsibility for her. He surveyed the throng of people ahead to catch a glimpse of her. Carrying Maddy on her hip, she accompanied Mrs. Herron and a group of other ladies from the quilting club.

For the rest of the afternoon, people streamed back and forth between the sanctuary and the parish house, owned by one of Sage Creek's oldest residents. Still others gathered on the church lawn.

Caden offered condolences to Mrs. Wallow, and Stephanie shared her gratitude for the opportunity he'd given her. Then, noting the growing line behind them, they politely excused themselves and migrated to the food lining Doris's counters. She lived in the parish house next to the church and often hosted community events.

Filling his plate, he breathed in the scent of cheesy potato, baked peach and fried chicken wafting from the dishes spread before him. "Now's when we wish we hadn't stopped for lunch earlier, huh?"

Stephanie smiled. "Like Mrs. Herron says, there's always room for a slice of home-baked pie."

"And a smidge of Lucy's King Ranch chicken, and a small spoonful of pistachio salad…"

She laughed and followed his example, but with smaller, almost meager, portions.

"Where's your little sunshine?"

"With Mrs. Herron somewhere."

"Entertaining everyone, I'm sure." The child would bring moments of joy to an otherwise painful day.

He grabbed some napkins and cutlery and guided Stephanie to the church's picnic table beneath the shade of an old oak tree. The gentle breeze stirred loose strands of her hair, carrying with it her soft floral scent.

Suddenly, the two of them sitting alone in the shade felt much too intimate.

He shifted. "Surprising no one snatched this spot yet." He half hoped others would join them, but also that they wouldn't. "Can I get you something to drink?"

"Oh, I can grab a soda. But thank you."

"I'll get it." He hurried off before she could protest.

He felt ridiculous, like an immature schoolboy who sidled up to his crush, then became tongue-tied.

A group of men were gathered around the open cooler. They expressed sympathy for Dr. Wallow's death and concern for the veterinary practice.

"I was blessed to work under the man for the past nine years," Caden said. "He taught me a great deal. About animal care and running an efficient clinic. And about integrity, compassion and the importance of laughter."

Drake Owens, an old football buddy, nodded. "That guy was such a prankster. He had a joke for everything."

He shoved a hand in his pocket. "You planning on hiring anyone?"

"Hope to. Figured I'd start with a relief vet first." He needed to get a better grasp on the clinic finances, which Dr. Wallow had handled, to decide on a long-term salary. One that was competitive enough to attract competent help without draining their account.

Could he afford another vet *and* a technician? If he tightened their budget in other areas, maybe. Better question— was that what was best for the clinic?

He forced a smile. "Guess I best grab those Cokes I came for, before the youth guzzle them all."

The guys laughed and sent him off with a handshake and invitations to call should he need anything.

He thanked them, then, with two chilled drinks, headed back to the picnic table. He halted mid-step. Gabe Johnson, a former friend from high school, emphasis on former, who'd stolen his high school girlfriend, was talking with Stephanie, no doubt trying to get his hooks in her.

Some people never change.

Jaw tense, Caden strode toward them.

Stephanie glanced up, and her gentle smile only made him want to chase the guy off all the more.

Gabe rotated to face him. "Hey, Doc. Sorry for your loss."

Caden gave Stephanie her drink. "Thank you." Even if the sentiment felt hollow.

The man initiated small talk for a moment then, one hand in his pocket, turned back toward Stephanie. "Any chance you're free tomorrow night?"

She picked at a cuticle, then took in a visible breath. "I've got plans."

"Sunday, then?"

"Weekends are really tight."

He raised his hands, palms out. "Hey, I get it. You don't

know me from Adam. How about you give me your number? So we can become more familiar with each other."

When she didn't respond, he said, "Better yet, I'll give you mine." Obviously undaunted by her rejection, Gabe patted his pockets. "I'll be right back."

Frowning, Caden watched him leave.

"You okay?" Stephanie regarded him with a furrowed brow.

He nodded. "Let's just say I know the guy. Unfortunately."

Her expression suggested his animosity toward Gabe had surprised her.

The prick of jealousy he'd felt upon seeing her talking to Gabe had surprised and concerned him, as well.

Chapter Six

Sunday morning, Mr. Herron followed a gray station wagon into Faith Trinity's lot. Stephanie tried to settle her thoughts by focusing on all the families heading toward the church. They all appeared so peaceful, as if they hadn't a care in the world.

She envied that. Did their inner calm come from their faith, or were their lives simpler and more predictable than hers?

She rubbed her triceps. John, paroled. She knew this day was coming, but that didn't make the news any easier.

"Let's get our worship on, ladies." Vincent grinned, cut the engine and stepped out of the vehicle. Adjusting his hat, he quickly became engaged in a conversation with an older couple who'd pulled in near the same time.

From the front seat, Cassandra swiveled to face Stephanie. "You going to be okay, sugar?" She squeezed her hand. "You look as tense as a pup at bath time."

Stephanie forced a wobbly smile. "Absolutely."

"Don't you worry none. These folks are as relaxed as they come." She motioned toward the church. "You don't have to know any special words, or even sing the hymns if you don't want. Just come in, find your place next to me and soak up all of God's love."

Cassandra always seemed to know just what to say.

Maddy, wearing a pink dress with ruffled trim Cassandra had bought her, started whining and tugging at her car seat straps. "Out, pwease!"

Stephanie laughed. "Alright, sweetie. I hear you."

She went to her daughter's door, lifted her out, wrapped her in a tight hug and deposited her on her feet. Then the three of them crossed the lot hand in hand, Maddy skip-bouncing in the middle.

Whistling, Vincent fell into step beside his wife. "Sure is a beautiful day, isn't it, love?" He looked at Cassandra with the adoration Stephanie had once believed only occurred in fairy tales.

But then she met the Herrons. If she ever did open her heart to a man again, she wanted one who gazed at her with the same devotion Vincent had for Cassandra. As if she were the most beautiful woman he'd ever seen.

Cassandra smiled. "Nice enough for a picnic, I'd say."

"I get stories?" Maddy peered up at the woman who was quickly becoming an adoptive grandmother.

"In Sunday school?" Cassandra nodded. "Plus, you'll learn songs with hand motions, will get to color a coloring page—"

"With pink and purple?"

"I don't rightly know what crayons they've got." Cassandra angled her head. "Probably depends on how many have been broken. But if they've got pink and purple, certainly."

Near the entrance, Maddy wiggled free from their grip and, reaching high to grasp the railing, clambered up the steps.

"Wait for Mama." Stephanie hustled after her, catching her just as she entered the crowded foyer.

"Good morning."

Her heart skipped at the sound of Caden's deep yet

gentle voice. Smoothing her windblown hair, she straightened. "Hi."

Freshly shaven and dressed in a short-sleeved blue-and-green-striped button-down shirt, he looked much too attractive. "Hey, there, princess." He held his hand out.

Maddy stared at it for a moment before giving him a high five, clearly using every ounce of oomph she had.

He laughed, then shifted his dancing eyes to Stephanie. "Haven't seen you in forever." His wink sent a jolt through her, a reaction that once again initiated caution. A caution she'd started to think was unnecessary—until the memorial service.

He'd seemed jealous Gabe was talking to her. While she may have misread him, her experience with John had taught her to pay attention to every potential red flag, however slight.

Cassandra joined them. "Good to see you, Caden. You sitting with us this morning?"

His cheeks colored, and he seemed to hesitate. "I appreciate the offer, ma'am, and it's not that I don't want to or anything. But you know how my mama is about having all her kids and grandkids close by during worship."

"Don't blame her one bit." She smiled, then someone must've caught her eye, because she looped an arm through Stephanie's and tugged her forward. "Come and meet the ladies."

So much for slipping in and out unnoticed.

Stephanie placed Maddy on her hip and followed Cassandra past the back rows, where she would've loved to hide. They continued to three pews from the front where two older couples sat. She recognized Lucy from the day at the boutique.

"Lookee here." Lucy stood to greet them. "How is the little cutie pie?"

Maddy pulled back, and Stephanie gave her a gentle hug.

"You've met?" Cassandra asked.

Lucy nodded and patted Maddy's cheek. "You know we've got a nursery with toys and rockers and all that."

"The princess was all set to go but then turned shy once we started to leave. I told Stephanie no one would mind if the child stayed with us this morning." Cassandra rubbed Maddy's back.

"Well, she sure is a cutie." Lucy smoothed a hand over the girl's head. "I don't remember if you told me her age. She's, what? Three?"

Stephanie nodded.

"You survived the terrible twos, huh?" She chuckled.

"Guess so." Not that Maddy had ever given her much trouble, in that regard. She'd always been fairly quiet and agreeable. Happy. A constant source of joy amid all Stephanie's challenges. Her daughter's giggles and bright, laughing eyes had carried Stephanie through all those nights at the shelter.

"Boy, do I remember those days." Lucy launched into a story about one of her grandsons who, apparently, had enough vinegar to pickle her whole garden. "Then there was little Charlotte. That girl."

By the time service started, Stephanie was certain she'd learned about each of Lucy's grandchildren. She should've known Cassandra's friends would be as kind and accepting as she was. In fact, nearly all of Sage Creek seemed that way. Dr. Wallow had insisted this was a great place to raise kids. It appeared he was right.

The pastor told a story about a widow who nearly starved to death during a time of famine. "God saw that woman, her son, their need, and He met it through Elijah."

He made eye contact with a few congregants. "We've all been that mother, haven't we? Maybe we're her now—standing in a place of need, hoping God will send someone to help. Then comes the time when we're Elijahs—when

God's telling us to act. Be that friend, take that meal, buy your neighbor that tank of gas. Because we're family, and that's what families do. We lean on one another."

She glanced to Caden, sitting kitty-corner a few rows up. Though initially reluctant regarding her internship, he'd been kind and patient with her. He seemed to genuinely want her to succeed. Of course, she'd be even more grateful if he offered her full-time employment. Maybe God could stir his heart to offer her a steady position? Was that what the pastor meant about using people to meet needs?

After service, Cassandra handed Stephanie an opened bulletin and tapped a paragraph three-quarters of the way down. "You should go."

Stephanie read the text. *Women's Connection.* "What is it?"

"A group of ladies meet to talk, craft, sometimes discuss books or Bible studies. It'd be a great place to form relationships and build something of a support system, which we *all* need."

She chewed her bottom lip. "I don't know."

"Just give it a try. Seems to me you've got nothing to lose and a whole lot to gain. Although you'll need to bring little miss, as Vincent and I've got a peach festival meeting this evening. But they've got childcare. Matter of fact, that might be a great way for Maddy to make some friends."

Standing in the foyer, Caden watched Stephanie with some of the ladies from the quilting group. Her turquoise dress, gathered at her trim waist, brought out her skin's pink undertones. Her long silky black hair cascaded over her delicate shoulders, and when she laughed, her smile lit her face.

She was more relaxed than he'd seen her. Except for when she was with one of their patients, at least, when she didn't realize he was watching her. The moment he walked into the room, however, she tensed up and seemed to tune immediately to him. Almost like he was grading her or something.

Then again, he sort of was.

First thing tomorrow, he'd crunch the numbers again, cut expenses and free up funds for payroll—enough to hire a vet *and* Stephanie.

Only because Stephanie was great with the animals. The fact that his pulse quickened whenever she turned those soft blue eyes his way had nothing to do with it. He'd experienced enough heartache after Renée and wasn't looking for a repeat.

"Hey there."

A hand clamped on his shoulder, and he turned to see Pastor Roger standing beside him.

"Great sermon."

"I was hoping you'd say that."

Caden raised an eyebrow. "Something tells me I won't like where this is headed."

"Sure you will. You always want to put feet to your faith, am I right?"

He moved aside to let a few teenagers past. "What do you need?"

"Our ladies group meets tonight, and we're short on childcare."

He raised his hands, palms out. "I don't know the first thing about changing a diaper or burping a baby."

"Don't worry, most of the kids are potty-trained. Besides, you did great last month during VBS."

"That's because I served on the snack crew. All I had to do was hand out juice and cookies." That had practically made him every child's new best friend. "Not even I could mess that up."

Pastor Roger laughed. "Aislyn from youth group will be there. She's amazing and could handle the kiddos herself.

But church policy says we always need two people, one of them an adult, in a room."

He scratched his neck. "What time?"

"See you at seven." Roger grinned, gave his shoulder another squeeze and left.

Caden sighed. So much for watching the ball game, but Pastor was right. This would give Caden an opportunity to live out today's message.

His gaze shifted back to Stephanie, then to her daughter, standing beside her. That little thing sure was cute and already a spitting image of her mama.

She'd turn a lot of heads one day. Like Stephanie had, no doubt.

Like Stephanie still did.

He thought back to the memorial service and how quickly Gabe Johnson had tried to move in on her. Had she called him? He'd given her his number.

Why did Caden care so much?

As her boss, he was probably feeling a big-brother protectiveness over her. Plus, she was new in town. It made sense he'd feel obligated to watch over her. And *not* because he was falling for her. He needed a relationship right now like he needed a whack to the head—which was precisely where his past relationship had landed him. Not to mention she had a kid, one he could easily see himself growing attached to, and potentially, her to him.

Even contemplating dating her, which he most certainly wasn't, felt emotionally dangerous to all involved.

His phone beeped a text, and he glanced at the screen. His mom was inviting him to dinner.

He shot her a quick reply, explaining his commitment. I'd love to stop by, but unfortunately, I'm going to have to take a raincheck.

His mom loved having him and his siblings over for Sunday supper. She'd started the tradition when his oldest brother had first moved out, likely as a way to remain connected. Caden was grateful for that. For his mom's home cooking and for all the conversations and laughter still spent around that old kitchen table, the place of so many memories.

Meals at his place tended to be microwaved food eaten alone in front of the television. His table had become something of a catch-all area. The place he deposited whatever he came in with or wanted to deal with later.

The clutter revealed his nonexistent social life.

If he had more time and wasn't Stephanie's boss, then maybe he'd invite her over for a cup of coffee.

Thinking that way would only further complicate things. With a mental shake, he dashed out of the church, tipping his hat at folks as he passed, and to his truck.

He had just enough time to run home and scarf down some canned stew before returning to the church. Once there, he followed the sound of laughing children toward the classrooms in the back.

Turning down the short hall, he nearly ran into Stephanie.

"Excuse me." He stepped back, a surge of warmth sweeping through him.

She'd changed into soft pink shorts and a matching top that accentuated her curves.

Her gaze faltered slightly, and she tucked a lock of hair behind her ears. "Hi."

"You here for the ladies' group?"

She offered a beautifully shy smile and nodded.

"Y'all making something crafty?"

"I'm not really sure. This is my first time."

Duh. He should've known that, considering she was new to town. Did her being here mean she was putting down roots? And if so, that she'd put all her eggs in the clinic's basket? He worried she'd be crushed if he didn't hire her.

But surely she knew how shaky his finances were. True, in losing Wallow, they'd lost the expense of his salary, but depending on how many appointments Caden needed to cut, they could also forfeit a chunk of income.

Hopefully he'd find another vet soon.

Of course, that also meant he'd need to clear his already overfilled schedule for interviews.

"Hi!" He turned to see Kayla Williams striding toward them with a wide smile. She greeted Caden with a nod, then introduced herself to Stephanie. "You must be Stephanie Thornton."

Stephanie nodded.

"Ms. Cassandra said you might be coming. I'm glad you did." Kayla's kind eyes always had a way of giving people a hug. "Doris Harper's opened her doors to us. You remember her from Doc Wallow's wake? She lets us use her living room. Says it gives her an excuse to bake, which is one of her greatest passions, and a great fit for us. We ladies can eat." She laughed, then eyed Stephanie with exaggerated seriousness. "You do like coffee, correct?"

Stephanie smiled. "Absolutely."

"Then we can be friends." Kayla's grin returned. "I was just heading to the bathroom, but if you wait, I can walk you over."

"I can take her." His sudden desire to extend his time with her triggered all sorts of warning bells.

Cool it, Caden.

"Great," she said. "There's fresh coffee and some pastries that almost look much too pretty to eat. But of course, we can't let them go to waste. Help yourself, and I'll be there in a minute."

They nodded goodbye, then Caden led Stephanie back through the sanctuary and down the hall toward the parish house.

He stepped into the early evening sun. "Did y'all have women's get-togethers at your old church?"

"I didn't go to church much."

"Oh." Another reason Caden shouldn't even entertain thoughts of dating her. He'd watched a friend get involved with a nonbeliever, saw firsthand the conflict that often came when two worldviews collided.

Yet Stephanie had come to worship service this morning, and she was here now, presumably trying to make Christian friends. Maybe she'd resolved whatever had kept her from church?

They crossed the short expanse of lawn to Doris's place. Through the window, he saw a handful of women from his Sunday school class along with half a dozen or so he recognized from around town. About half the ladies were stitching or crocheting while they sat and talked. The others were laughing and eating.

He rotated toward Stephanie with a low whistle. "Y'all got some good eats up in there. I'm almost tempted to ask you to sneak me out a slice of zebra brownies that I'm near certain Lucy made. That woman can bake."

"Maybe I can stash a platter or two in my purse." Her eyes twinkled with mischief.

"Or, if you're hankering for something sugar-loaded, we can meet at the Sweet Spot sometime." Heat flooded his face. Had he really said that—practically asked her on a date?

Hopefully she'd take his blunder as a joke, which surely it was.

Because beautiful or not, he and Stephanie could *not* date. For numerous reasons.

But that didn't mean he couldn't be friendly and maybe even offer to show her around town. Being as she was new, she was probably lonely. Everyone needed support and encouragement. It certainly couldn't be easy, being a single mom interning at a busy, and temporarily chaotic, veterinary clinic. Seemed only right, gentlemanly, to come alongside her—in a professional, friendly way, of course.

What if he couldn't hire her? Then God would provide her with work elsewhere.

And if she did stay on at the clinic? Then she'd be off-limits, romantically speaking, for sure.

He suppressed a sigh. This situation was becoming more complicated and confusing by the day.

Standing on Doris's stoop, she seemed hesitant, almost nervous. Her vulnerability stirred his protective side.

"Don't worry. These ladies are about as kind and accepting as they come. And I'm sure Margie and Lucy will show up at some point. They always do. Those two could've coined the phrase, 'never knew a stranger.'"

She smiled. "I'm a grown-up."

"And a strong and determined one at that."

He felt like she needed to hear that. He didn't know her story but sensed she'd been beaten down at some point and was trying to rediscover her wings. Maybe, in some small way, he could help her—whether or not he hired her.

She studied him, as if surprised by his statement.

"Anyone who has the gumption to travel halfway across the country for an internship obviously has grit." He felt certain she must've overcome a lot, otherwise she wouldn't be here, at this meeting, nor at the Herrons'. "A woman like that won't let anything slow her down or knock her back, am I right?"

"Thank you for the encouragement." Chin slightly raised, she rang the bell.

"Guess I'll leave you to it." He tipped his hat and walked away.

The door creaked open and someone's cheerful voice followed.

Whatever had brought her to Sage Creek, and whatever

she still had to conquer, she'd be in good hands. Especially with Kayla leading the ladies' group. She practically exploded with the love and grace of Christ.

Inside the sanctuary, he paused to bow his head. *Help me do the same, Lord. To display Your love, to Stephanie especially. I don't know why You brought her here, but You did. More than anything, I want to serve You. To be the type of man that brings help, hope and healing to those in need, just like Pastor Roger urged this morning.*

Just don't let me become emotionally entangled with the woman.

What about Caden's desire for a family? Did his profession negate that? Dr. Wallow had made things work. If only he were still alive for Caden to ask how. Not that he had any intention of dating Stephanie, regardless of the effect she had on him. But neither could the clinic become his entire life.

He returned to the kids' classroom to find the children engaged in a game of duck, duck, goose. Maddy was clearly confused. Whenever the boy circling the others tapped her head, she shrank back and frowned at him intensely as he continued.

The boy bonked a blonde girl on the head, yelled, "Goose," and ran.

All the others did, as well.

Laughing, he helped Aislyn corral the little ones back to the circle. After about the third time of this, they gave up and allowed the younger ones to toddle off toward the activity stations positioned around the room.

Aislyn tossed a beanbag into a bucket. "Want to let them free play for a bit? And if they get bored, play a movie?"

"Sounds good."

He spent the rest of the evening alternating between playing blocks, cars and blowing bubbles, a favorite activity among the toddlers. But even then, their attention span lasted five minutes tops before they darted off to something else. He'd just returned a smattering of vehicles to their container when Maddy approached with a book in hand.

"Read to me?" Her big blue eyes, peering up at him, melted his heart.

"Definitely." He led her to the table and sat, expecting her to take the chair beside him. Instead, she climbed into his lap. He stiffened, then relaxed and, holding the book in one hand, wrapped his free arm around her.

"Isn't she adorable?" Aislyn grinned.

She and her mama both, and that could be a problem.

Chapter Seven

Maddy fell asleep on the drive home from the women's group, deep enough that Stephanie was able to carry her inside and tuck her into bed without waking her. Needing a moment to process, she headed into the kitchen to find Cassandra sitting at the table with two steaming mugs of hot cocoa.

The sweet gesture felt like balm to Stephanie's anxious heart. "Thank you." She sat across from her and took the cup she offered.

"How'd it go?"

"I'm not sure how to answer that."

"Did something happen?"

"No. It's just... I'm thinking about something one of the girls shared."

"Something triggering?"

"A little."

"Healing takes time." She placed a hand on Stephanie's arm. "How'd Maddy do in childcare?"

"Good." She chewed her bottom lip, unsure how much she wanted to verbalize. Not sure she could express it all. Walking in to see Maddy sitting on Caden's lap, the tenderness he'd displayed, had pricked two related and deeply buried longings.

She'd so wanted a father growing up, someone to treat her like a princess, to fight for her, to see and call out the best in her. She wanted that for Maddy even more, but she wasn't sure she had the courage to become involved with another man. Or the wisdom to know if he was worthy of her daughter's affections.

"I know in my head that Maddy and I are safe." She rubbed the back of her arm and relayed what her mother had told her the day she'd gone shopping. "But I felt so much better when John was safely locked behind bars."

She hated that he could still make her feel so afraid. She needed to move on, focus on making a new life for her and Maddy.

Why did their future still feel so precarious?

"I imagine it'll take time before you truly feel safe again." Cassandra's eyes radiated compassion. "It's a process. But getting out and meeting folks will help. That, my girl, is why you're here. To learn to live again."

"I really appreciate how you're investing in me." She cherished times like this.

Mrs. Herron's mentorship played a significant role in her journey.

She'd hoped her time at the clinic would, as well. Unfortunately, Caden simply didn't have time to fulfill all of Dr. Wallow's promises. The man barely paused long enough for lunch most days, it seemed. And if, after her internship ended, she found herself without a job and had to move in with her mom?

Maddy would love that.

But she'd miss the Herrons, too, as would Stephanie. Besides, her mom's place was super small, which meant one of them would have to sleep on the couch. And because she worked full time, Stephanie would need to pay for childcare. That might cost more than she could afford.

Then there was the whole problem of getting there. Traveling halfway across the country was exhausting, hard on Maddy and expensive.

"Trust, sweet girl." Cassandra softly patted Stephanie's cheek. "God's got you and that precious little one of yours." She pushed up from the table. "I best get some rest. Tomorrow will hit me soon enough." Chuckling, she shuffled off.

Stephanie remained where she was, contemplating all Cassandra had said, not just tonight, but in numerous conversations since her and Maddy's arrival. She spoke of God's care and attentiveness, as if they were things a person could count on. What would it be like to live with such assurance?

She placed her mug in the sink and migrated to the living room. Cassandra's Bible sat on the coffee table with numerous bookmarks protruding from the pages.

Stephanie picked it up and ran her hand across the smooth, worn leather, then opened to the first bookmark. The bold subheading read: *Manna from Heaven.* In the margin, Cassandra had written: *God supplied what they needed for that day. Trust God's provisions.*

Stephanie could understand why God would provide for the Herrons. They were kind and generous, worked hard. Made wise choices.

Would He provide for Stephanie, as well? Even if the job at the clinic didn't come through and she'd made a huge mistake in coming here? Granted, her training would still help, but she'd be back to job hunting.

And if not for her, then for Maddy?

She thought of the phrase *what they needed for that day.*

While she didn't know what tomorrow held, today, she and Maddy had food, shelter and support from a couple who treated them both like family.

Had God given her those things?

Returning the Bible, she stood and slipped out onto the porch, her favorite thinking spot. An owl hooted in the distance over the symphony of chirping crickets. The sky was lit with countless shimmering stars, and a nearly full moon cast the orchard in a silvery glow.

"I miss you, Mom." While she loved having Cassandra to talk to, it simply wasn't the same.

Was her mom still awake? She doubted it but shot her a Facebook message asking just in case. Her cell vibrated an incoming call almost immediately.

She answered with a smile. "Hi." Separated by over a thousand miles, it felt like they hadn't spoken in forever, although it'd only been a few days.

"Is everything alright?"

"I guess I'm processing." She sat in one of the rockers.

"Processing is good." Her voice carried warmth.

Stephanie told her about her evening. "The ladies were super nice. But there was this one woman… She used to be in an abusive relationship. She left the guy a year ago and recently started dating again."

She thought back to that conversation and all the emotions that had played on the woman's face. "She seemed so…conflicted. Listening to her talk, I sensed she knows her new boyfriend is bad news but is trying to convince herself otherwise. The poor woman kept jockeying between common sense and a lovestruck school girl. In the end, she firmly stated, probably to convince herself, that she was smart enough to proceed with caution."

"When she needs to run fast in the other direction?"

"From the sounds of it."

"Loneliness can cause people to deceive themselves into believing good is bad and bad is good."

"And to assume every concern is an overreaction. I get it. I've been there." While she'd promised herself never to let a man charm her into an abusive relationship ever again, she worried.

She would do whatever it took to keep Maddy safe, even

if that meant remaining single for the rest of her life. Hopefully it wouldn't come to that.

"I see." Her mother paused long enough to suggest she shared some of Stephanie's questions and concerns. "What's his name?"

An image of Caden flashed to mind, sending a flutter through her midsection. "It's not that. I'm just trying to figure out how to know when I'm ready. Not just to date, but to date well. I don't want to end up like that woman, you know? It sounded like she's landed right back where she started but with a different man."

"You want to know how to avoid getting involved with another John."

She released a breath. "Right. I mean, he seemed so nice in the beginning. So attentive, so caring and protective." She sensed those same qualities in Caden, along with a quiet strength that drew her to him.

John had been strong, too, but he'd rarely displayed that in quiet ways.

"Maybe a little too protective? Bordering on possessive?"

"I can see that now, but I'm not sure I would've recognized that back then."

"Recognized or admitted it?"

She frowned. "I get what you're saying, but that sort of proves my point. Looking back, I can totally see all the red flags I should've been more alert to. Only I was so infatuated by John, and maybe by the idea of getting married, that I downplayed them all."

"You're much stronger and wiser now. You still worried about him finding you both? Now that he's paroled?"

She traced her finger along a groove in the armrest. "Sometimes I get a burst of anxiety, but I know we're safe here. The more I remind myself of that, the less afraid I feel."

"That's good. Progress."

"Only now I have a new fear."

"Yes?"

"I'm worried my longing for Maddy to have a daddy—" and a lifelong companion for herself, for that romance her childhood storybooks always promised "—might distort my perception."

"So, pray. And talk with Ms. Cassandra. I get the feeling she's pretty wise regarding these things. And take it slow."

"Yeah." Slow still implied forward movement, right?

Her mom laughed. "Alright, now tell me about this Texan."

Stephanie wasn't ready to do that. She worried voicing her emotions would give them strength. She was having a difficult enough time keeping her feelings regarding Caden in check as it was. So instead, she shifted the conversation to surprising, and occasionally hilarious, animal experiences.

By the time their call ended, she'd laughed herself into a bellyache. Thoughts quieted, she went to bed and soon fell asleep to the soft, rhythmic sound of her daughter's breathing as she slept.

The next morning, her alarm woke her much too early, which would make her longer-than-normal day challenging. She was, however, looking forward to seeing Caden.

Normally, she would've redirected her thinking, but her conversation with her mom had reignited her original question.

Was she maybe ready to date? It had been three years since she left her husband, after all, and she'd spent considerable time in therapy. She'd learned how to evaluate her feelings, set boundaries and recognize warning signs in potential abusers. She'd even begun to anticipate her future again, believing she did indeed have a future. What's more, she'd been actively pursuing her dreams for some time.

Surely that meant something.

Standing in front of her bedroom mirror, she primped, then spritzed her hair while Maddy played and sang on the floor behind her.

Her thoughts drifted to the night before, to when she'd walked into the children's room to see Maddy sitting on Caden's lap, looking so relaxed. So happy. Caden's eyes had lit with laughter as he read from the storybook he'd been holding, his voice rising and falling with each character. They'd both appeared completely lost in that moment, and Stephanie had felt reluctant to interrupt them.

Them sitting together like that, Caden acting so gentle and tender and Maddy looking so relaxed? That was how she'd always dreamed the perfect father-daughter relationship would look.

From everything she'd seen, Caden would make a great dad.

She almost laughed out loud. What was she doing, going from a night of babysitting to fantasies about happily-ever-after?

Stephanie wasn't even sure she'd have a job by the time her internship was over, let alone where things might stand between her and Caden.

Still, this new stage felt good. All her emotions suggested maybe she was starting to find herself again.

Southern gospel drifted from the kitchen where, based on the clanking of pans, Cassandra was making breakfast. Her voice rose and fell with the music. She sang of a hope greater than the worst storms and a life nothing could snuff out.

Stephanie paused and closed her eyes. "I want that, God."

The smell of bacon and yeasty cinnamon made her stomach rumble loud enough to make Maddy giggle.

"Was that funny?" Stephanie swept her up and gave her

a squeeze. "How's your tummy this morning?" She blew a raspberry into Maddy's neck, turning her giggles into high-pitched squeals. "You hungry?"

"Nummies?"

"Sure smells like it." Feeling lighter than she had since arriving in Sage Creek, she carried Maddy into the kitchen.

Cassandra stood at the counter dishing steaming cinnamon rolls onto a cooling rack. "Good morning." She wiped her hands on a dish towel and greeted Stephanie with a side hug and Maddy with a tickle under the chin. "Hey, there, peanut. How would you like to drizzle the icing?"

Maddy nodded and wiggled out of Stephanie's arms. She tried to climb onto the chair before Cassandra had fully pulled it to the counter.

"Hold on, little one." She laughed. With the chair in place, she helped Maddy onto it and positioned the bowl of icing in front of her. "Just scoop some up and pour it over the rolls, like this." She demonstrated while Maddy watched with big eyes. "You got it?"

Licking her lips, Maddy nodded again.

Cassandra smiled at Stephanie. "Help yourself, sugar. They're fresh out of the oven. Orange juice, peach slices and a platter of cooked bacon are on the table. Vincent won't be joining us. He headed out to the orchard sometime before the rooster found his voice. That'll probably be his MO until the end of peach season."

"Did you need my help this evening?"

Cassandra waved a hand. "You focus on doing what you came for and taking care of your little nugget. I almost forgot. The county animal shelter is looking to add to their staff. It's not a vet tech position, but maybe it could lead to something. And Vincent suggested you stop by Hill Country Feed and Grain. Check the community board to see if any local ranchers are hiring. Might want to talk to Omar, the owner of the feed store. He about knows everyone and everything. I know your internship won't be over right quick, but figured you'd want something lined up for after. To ease your mind."

In case Caden cut her loose.

Stephanie smiled. "You know me well."

"Just understand what it's like to worry about an unknown future."

"Won't ranchers want a licensed vet?" Worse, she didn't exactly have a competitive résumé.

"Doubt anyone around here has the funds for that. But a lot of folks could use a hand from someone who knows their way around a stable or barn. By summer's end, you'll more than qualify. They might even have a missus who'll let your little one tag along with their kiddos."

Childcare always complicated things.

Was there any chance she and Maddy could stay here, at least until she saved enough to get herself started? Unfortunately, she didn't have the courage to ask. Not yet.

"Oh, my." Laughing, Cassandra pulled the wooden spoon, dripping with icing, from Maddy. Her face, hands and PJ top were a sticky mess. "I'm going to venture a guess and say I plumb stole Ms. Sweet Pea's appetite. Not to mention guaranteed her need for a bath." She eyed a glob of goo in the child's hair. "But don't let that trouble you none, Mama. This munchkin and I will be spending our morning chasing butterflies around the orchard and filling up on fresh peaches."

Stephanie smiled and deposited her now-empty plate in the dishwasher. "I'm not concerned in the slightest." What a nice feeling that was, knowing she had nothing to worry about as far as Maddy's care was concerned. Her anxiety regarding future employment, however, was another matter.

A snippet from Sunday's church message came to mind, soothing her. *"If you're in a place of need, trust that God sees you. He cares and has the power to turn your biggest problem into a miracle. Just keep filling your oil jars—doing whatever it is God's asking you to do—until He sends aid. His help will arrive right on time."*

Stephanie wanted to believe that. She wanted the same kind of faith she saw in Cassandra and Vincent. And Caden.

She glanced at the time on her phone. "I should get going."

Washing Maddy's sticky face and hands at the sink, Cassandra glanced over her shoulder, nodded and deposited the child on her feet. "How about we walk your mama out, then fill the tub with cotton candy bubbles and bath toys? Then off to the fields we'll go, to find us some pretties, right, kiddo?"

Stephanie smiled at Cassandra's use of Maddy's term for flowers. Though she knew and could say the proper word—replacing the *l* sound with a *w*—she preferred to use her own vocabulary. Blow flowers in place of dandelions, flutterbies for butterflies, nummies for food—at least, for food she enjoyed.

Mornings like this assured Stephanie she'd made the right decision coming here. She hated to think what their lives would be like now if she'd never found the courage to leave her ex.

Thankfully, that wasn't her story.

As usual, she arrived at the clinic to find Caden's truck in the driveway, the building's lights on and the front doors unlocked.

"Hello?" she called out as she entered. Caden didn't answer, so she crossed the lobby and peered down the hall. "Dr. Stoughton?"

"Back here."

She followed his voice to his office. He sat hunched over his desk, papers spread before her. His cowboy hat sat on the far corner on top of a binder.

He looked up when she entered, and the purple tint below his eyes indicated he hadn't gotten much sleep.

"How can I help?" she asked.

With a sigh, he raked a hand through his hair. For a moment, he seemed lost for words. Like his mind was playing catch-up. "You might have time to work more on our medicines before our first appointment."

"No problem."

He refocused on the papers in front of him, and she could sense his stress. Based on the old-school printing calculator he started punching into, she assumed he was working on office finances. His deep frown suggested they didn't look good.

Though she hoped otherwise, she feared that might hinder her future employment.

So she'd find a job elsewhere. She hadn't come this far to give up now, and she'd do whatever it took to give Maddy the life she deserved.

But would she still be able to see Caden?

The question sat heavier than she was ready to admit.

Chapter Eight

Caden eyed the medicine storage, then inside the locked fridge, pleased with how Stephanie had organized and cleaned it all. He deposited the inventory sheet on his desk to deal with over lunch and hurried down the hall to meet with his next patient.

Stephanie was waiting for him outside the exam room to catch him up to speed on a three-year-old Great Dane mix. "The owner detected an abnormal gait a few months ago, mostly when he ascended and descended their stairs. They thought he was being clumsy but then noticed signs he was getting worse."

"His awkwardness—always in the back legs?"

She nodded.

"Any noticeable difficulty rising from a lying position?"

"Yes."

"What are your thoughts?" He wanted her to think through the symptoms and suggest next steps. That was one of the best ways a person could learn.

"He didn't have an accident that they're aware of, and he's a large breed…" Her brows pinched together as she likely sifted through years of educational knowledge. She often seemed hesitant to get things wrong, as if worried he'd send her packing.

In reality, he needed to know she had the courage to act, even when uncertain. Veterinary medicine involved making the best decision possible based on what one knew, even if there remained a good deal one didn't. That was why people called it a practice. Sometimes answers seemed clear. Most times, not so much.

"Hip dysplasia?" She rubbed her collarbone. "Or wobbler syndrome."

"What would you suggest?"

"I'd want to see him walk, check his hip extension, watch for signs of pain."

"Good. Then what?"

"X-rays to rule out bone lesions or mimicking diseases."

"Excellent."

The way her face brightened, as if his approval meant the world to her, temporarily stalled his thinking. He cleared his throat to reorient himself. He needed to focus on his role as boss before his heart rebelled on him.

Although if he were to start dating again, he'd be lucky to find a girl like Stephanie. Smart, kind, hardworking. Treated each animal, including the ornery ones, with the same tenderness he'd seen her show her daughter.

"Doc?"

Neck heating, he glanced up to find both the client, a middle-aged woman with brown hair parted down the center, and Stephanie waiting on him.

"Let's see what we've got, shall we?" He swept past her, catching a whiff of her sweet floral scent, and led the way to the exam room. He held the door open for both ladies, then followed them in. Stephanie remained standing near the counter. His client sat in the corner chair.

"Good morning, Mrs. Downing." He crossed the room and shook her hand. "Hello, Duke, ol' boy." He scratched the gentle giant behind the ears, laughing when the dog leaned into his hand. "Always the attention hog."

Mrs. Downing nodded, and the countless lines splayed across her forehead softened some. But her eyes remained alert, anxious. "He thinks he's part lap dog, part human."

Caden chuckled. Just like a Great Dane, perhaps the biggest cuddlers around. "Sounds about right."

She rubbed her thumb knuckle. "He really liked Dr. Wallow."

In other words, she wished he were still around, probably now more than ever. Caden had picked up on similar sentiments from other clients, as well. He couldn't blame them. Wallow had been older, more experienced, with a keen mind for business and oversight of the clinic.

Despite all of Caden's years as a practicing vet, people probably wondered if he could manage on his own. As much as he hated feeling the need to prove himself yet again, he understood the increased importance of managing the clinic well.

To allay Mrs. Downing's worries and build client-to-vet trust, he asked some additional questions interspersed with chitchat. He sensed Stephanie watching him, which made sense. She was here to learn, after all. But somehow, her standing there, gaze locked on him, felt different. In ways he couldn't analyze right now.

And later? Was Stephanie even interested?

Stop it.

He refocused on the dog. "How about I take a look?" He gently scooped the Dane up and placed him on the examination table.

By the time he finished, he felt certain the poor guy suffered from a neurological problem. Voice soft, he explained his suspicions to Mrs. Downing. "I'd need to perform imaging tests to be sure. Depending on what we find, we may need to do an MRI. Since he's not likely to sit still for that, we'd need to place him under general anesthesia."

"If it's wobbles, or whatever you called it?"

"We'll start him with anti-inflammatory medicine first. If that doesn't work, we'll discuss surgery."

"That sounds expensive."

Unfortunately, it was. "We can talk about payment options."

His gaze flickered to Stephanie. Her expression radiated compassion. She really loved these animals. If hired, she'd do her job well, so long as she didn't have any issues he wasn't aware of.

He hated to think this way, but he needed to remain alert.

Or was that a smokescreen? A way to protect his heart from getting hurt again?

At lunchtime, Stephanie grabbed her sandwich and ate on the drive to Hill Country Feed and Grain. Cassandra had texted their address along with a Bible verse about praying instead of worrying.

If only it were that easy. And yet... Stopped at the intersection of Main and B Street, she gazed at the pale blue sky streaked with wisps of clouds.

"God, I know I haven't talked to You in a while." Not since she'd started dating John, actually. "I realize I don't have the right to ask for anything, but I could really use a job. I'd love to stay on at the veterinary clinic..." An image of Caden's kind, laughing eyes flashed through her mind.

She released a breath. "Like I said, I'd love to stay where I'm at, but I'm not in a place to be picky. So long as I can support me and Maddy, I'll be happy. And oh so grateful."

Hill Country Feed and Grain sat about five minutes outside of town bordered by a wheat field on the right and tall cornstalks on the left. A handful of cars dotted the lot, most of them trucks. The vetmobile she'd heard Lisa complain about occupied a stall near the entrance.

Lisa made it seem as if the woman who ran the business was targeting Sage Creek Veterinary clients in underhanded ways. While Stephanie suspected she was exaggerating, she understood her apprehension. The clinic had been hit with a lot, leaving clients and staff unsettled to say the least. The impact of Dr. Wallow's death could easily fracture any cracks the clinic had prior.

Was Caden business-savvy enough to navigate it all?

As Stephanie stepped out of her air-conditioned vehicle, an image in her peripheral vision made her jump. Hand on her door handle, she whipped her head in that direction, struggling for air. It took a moment for the image of the man to register.

It wasn't John. Of course it wouldn't be.

She released a breath, then followed a short hunchbacked man into the warehouse-like structure. Inside smelled like fertilizer, dog food and something sweet she couldn't place. Aisles of crude shelving filled with massive bags stretched before her, and stacked buckets of varying sizes occupied the shelves to her left.

"Hello." An older gentleman in a ball cap and a large red apron greeted her with a smile. "Welcome to Hill Country Feed and Grain. How can I help you?" His name tag said Omar Luntz.

"Sir." She introduced herself, explained why she'd come and her role at the veterinary clinic.

He tugged on the skin beneath his neck. "You got experience with cattle?"

"I'm working with them now in my internship." No sense stating how little large animal experience she'd had prior.

"You wanting full-time?"

"Honestly, I'm open to anything. But I can't start until after summer."

"Come with me."

She followed him to a long, rectangular corkboard attached to the wall covered with flyers and slips of paper secured by thumbtacks. Someone was looking for a lost dog. Someone else wanted to sell a horse, and another resident was offering riding lessons.

"Tell you what." Omar pulled a pencil from behind his ear and removed a poster for an event dated two months prior. He wrote on the back of the page, then handed it over. "This here's my email. Send me your résumé. If I hear of anything, I'll pass your information on."

"Thank you." That wasn't exactly the lead she was hoping for, but it was better than nothing.

"My pleasure." He ambled off toward a woman trying to lift a twenty-five-pound bag of dog food into her cart.

Stephanie searched the mess of papers in front of her for help-wanted ads. There wasn't much. A local boarding facility wanted to hire an additional barn hand, probably to muck stalls and distribute hay. That would be labor-intensive, likely for little pay.

"Excuse me, ma'am."

She startled and turned to see a woman with shoulder-length blond hair standing beside her. "Oh, sorry." She moved aside to allow the woman a clearer visual of the board.

The lady stepped closer. "I'm Renée Elkins, owner of the Mobile TexaVet."

The person Lisa felt such animosity for. Stephanie doubted anyone operating out of a vehicle could sabotage Caden's practice, but she had no doubt the competition made things challenging. And every client lost, to the mobile vet and that new practice one town over, probably pricked Lisa's pride. Caden's body language whenever the woman was mentioned suggested he felt the same.

Stephanie smiled and introduced herself.

"Always good to meet another animal lover." Dr. Elkins's handshake felt more professional than friendly. "I'm not trying to be nosy, but I couldn't help overhearing your conversation with Omar."

"Okay?" Where was this headed?

"You looking for a job?"

"Potentially." She vaguely explained her current predicament, including her childcare challenges. Although she hated leading with that, considering some might view single parenting as a liability, she'd rather state her restrictions up front.

"It just so happens I'm looking to hire. Because I set my own hours, I can accommodate diverse scheduling needs." She explained her business. "Mostly I deal with small animals—dogs, cats, the occasional gerbil or guinea pig. I've doubled my clientele in the last week alone."

"I don't mean to sound rude, but...do you have enough business to hire additional staff?" Starting a career based on projected growth didn't feel stable. The flexibility certainly sounded appealing, however, as long as the pay allowed for childcare. Or the Herrons let her and Maddy stay.

"No pressure or commitment." Dr. Elkins handed over a business card. "Just an exploratory conversation between two professionals."

"It'd have to be in the evening."

"No problem."

As they discussed possible dates, Stephanie became nervous. This whole conversation felt wrong, like she was betraying Caden. "Can I get back to you?"

"Of course. Just give me a call." With a wave, Dr. Elkins headed toward the rear of the store.

The prospective backup plan encouraged Stephanie. But how would Caden feel about her working for his competition? Would that destroy any chance she had with him?

While the thought saddened her, she couldn't let him hinder her career. She'd been down that road before. When she finally had the courage to leave John, she'd determined to never again lose herself for a man.

Refocusing on the corkboard, she wrote down some leads, then hustled back to work. She arrived with five minutes to spare and pulled into the lot moments after a kid in a cherry-red coupe with a black stripe running from trunk to engine. When she parked beside him, she recognized the driver. It was Jeff, the volunteer she'd met the afternoon after her first on-site visits.

After eyeing Dr. Elkins's business card once more, she tucked it into her purse.

She'd feel so much more settled if she knew, once her internship ended, she'd secured long-term employment. Preferably here.

With a sigh, she gathered her things and stepped out into the humid air.

Jeff, now out of his car as well, turned to face her. "Hey." The kid's eyes were even more bloodshot than when she'd last seen him, the purple shadows more pronounced.

"Good to see you."

Dropping eye contact momentarily, he shifted his weight to his left foot. "Do y'all need any help? Walking boarders or something?"

"I'm not sure." Things had been busy, but the kid looked like he could use a nap, not a day at a chaotic clinic. Then again, everyone dealt with grief differently. Maybe his coping was to stay busy.

Seemed to be the way Caden had been handling his emotions.

"Doc Stoughton inside?"

"I imagine."

He gave a slight nod, crossed the lot, paused with his hand on the door, then entered.

Stephanie watched him for a moment, then followed into the considerably cooler clinic.

Jeff stood in the lobby, with one hand shoved in his pocket.

"I can get the doctor for you," she said.

He tapped his lips with the back of his hand, brow pinched. "Yeah, okay. Thanks."

"Jeff." Lisa's voice rose above the soft music filling the lobby. The wheels of her chair squeaked as she sprang to her feet. A moment later, she'd wrapped Jeff in a tight hug and was speaking soothing words to him.

Feeling like she was intruding on a private moment, Stephanie left to find the doctor. She stopped by the break room to deposit her lunch bag, then hurried out.

As she rounded the corner, she nearly collided with Caden.

"Sorry." His boyish smile tugged on her heart. "How was lunch?"

"Good." She had a feeling he'd worked through his. "Jeff's here to see you. He doesn't look so great."

Caden's expression immediately softened, and his shoulders seemed to wilt. "Probably needs someone to talk to. Although I wish he'd come in about thirty minutes ago, when I had more time to talk, I'm glad he's here."

"Actually, I think he wants to volunteer."

"Oh." He rubbed his forehead. "Guess I better find something for him to do."

"It might help him process his grief."

His expression indicated he didn't have the margin in his day to determine, then assign tasks for Jeff. The compassion in his eyes, however, suggested he'd figure something out.

With a quiet sigh, he turned toward the lobby, then paused. "You up for another on-site visit? We just got a call about a horse who had a rather rude introduction to a porcupine."

She winced. "That sounds painful."

"And challenging. The quills have barbs that tend to work themselves inward." He deposited his phone in his lab coat pocket. "Give me a few minutes to talk with Jeff, then we can head out." He turned to leave, then shifted back to face her. "Think you can get here a bit early tomorrow to go over our inventory with Lisa? The numbers seem off."

"Absolutely." Had she messed something up? She'd counted everything twice. "Off how?"

"Seems we've gone through some of our medications more than normal. Notably more."

Stephanie frowned. Just how disorganized was this clinic? Messing up an occasional appointment she could understand, but errors in their medication records? That could be a pretty big deal.

What if the clinic went under?

She followed him down the hall, then lingered near the reception desk while Caden and Jeff talked. The teen was acting strange, almost shifty. From grief? Most likely he was trying to maintain control of his emotions.

She used to do the same around John. He always assumed she was keeping something from him. And she had been, just not anything like he'd thought.

A few minutes later, Caden returned to the desk, Jeff accompanying. "Lisa, can you get Jeff the patient records from today?"

"Hard copies?"

"Yeah. He's going to check that they're complete. Make a list of what he needs to look for—date, that they're signed off. You know the drill."

"Sure thing."

"Call me if you need me." He touched Stephanie's arm, sending a jolt through her. "Shall we?"

Hoping the heat flooding her cheeks didn't show, she straightened. "Absolutely." Her reaction to Caden, which only seemed to intensify the more time she spent around him, concerned her. The last time a man had affected her this way, years of terror and pain had followed. She would not allow a repeat.

He held the clinic door open for her. "We'll want to be careful the quills don't break off when we try to remove them."

That was an experience she was *not* looking forward to. That poor horse!

Caden's mom pulled into the lot as they were exiting the building. She wore an orange visor over blond hair and was waving enthusiastically.

"You remember my mom?" Caden's tone conveyed obvious affection. "From the funeral?"

She nodded. "We didn't get a chance to talk much, but we met briefly."

He continued to his truck, deposited his vet bag in the back, then, with Stephanie standing beside him, waited for Mrs. Stoughton to approach.

She stepped out of her vehicle dressed in pink Bermuda shorts and yellow flip-flops, accented with large fabric flowers. Based on the vanilla-and-cinnamon scent wafting from the basket she carried, she'd brought goodies.

Caden grinned. "Hi, Mom."

"Sweetie." They hugged, then she handed him her basket. "Did some baking for my ladies' Bible study group and figured I'd make extra for my boys." She patted his cheek, then faced Stephanie. "It's good to see you again. I hope my son is treating you well."

"Ma'am." Stephanie extended her hand. "I'm grateful to be here."

Mrs. Stoughton captured it in both of hers with a warm smile. "Welcome to our little piece of paradise."

Caden peered into the container his mother handed him. "Macaroons, blueberry muffins… Are those cinnamon-raisin scones?"

She nodded. "Your favorite. I was hoping you'd have time for a quick midmorning coffee break, but I see you're heading out."

He briefly explained the reason. "Mina Anderson called it in. She said her parents left early this morning for Houston, and she hasn't been able to get a hold of them."

His mom shook her head. "Poor girl. She's what, fifteen now?"

"Thereabouts."

"I don't want to keep you. But before you both dash off…" She made eye contact with Stephanie. "It occurs to me I've not given you a proper Stoughton welcome. I'm guessing my son here hasn't, either." Arms crossed, she gave him a pointed look. "You free tonight? I'd love to have you over for dinner."

"Um…" A jolt shot through her, though whether at the thought of eating with strangers or spending an evening with her handsome boss, she wasn't sure. "I've got a daughter, and she can be a bit squiggly."

"Oh, I remember your little cutie from the funeral. Such a precious bundle of joy. Bring her. My grandkids will love the opportunity to make a friend. See you both at seven?"

Stephanie's gaze bounced between him and his mom, trying to gauge his reaction. This felt so intrusive, but it'd be rude to decline.

She gave a tentative nod.

"You're coming, too, right?" His mom flicked his arm. "I'm making a big ol' pot of chicken and dumplings."

Caden's stomach rumbled, and everyone laughed. "You know I'm always up for a home-cooked meal."

"Great." Mrs. Stoughton gave Stephanie what her mom had often called "a full-on mama hug," leaving her even more dazed. "I'm looking forward to spending time with you both. Make sure to come ready to eat." She laughed.

Then, with a wiggly-finger wave, she turned on her heel and pranced back to her vehicle.

Stephanie rubbed the back of her arm. How did Caden feel about this invite?

Then again, she had a feeling his mom's behavior hadn't surprised him. She seemed the type who often placed additional settings on her dinner table. As far as Stephanie could tell, that was the Sage Creek way. That was one of the things she loved most about this little town. It reminded her of the deep community she'd experienced back at the shelter.

Maddy would thrive in this small-town environment.

Caden opened then closed her door for her, rounded the vehicle and deposited the baked goods on the floorboard behind the driver's seat.

As he climbed in, the cab filled with the scent of his aftershave, or maybe his shampoo.

He turned the engine on and the radio off. "I hope you didn't feel bombarded a minute ago. If you don't want to go..."

"It's fine." Part of her indeed did want to go, and that worried her. She also knew better than to turn down an invite from her boss's mother.

Potential boss. But a night with his family could help move her in that direction. So long as she didn't do or say anything to mess things up. "Your mom's sweet, and based on the aroma wafting from that container she gave you, quite the baker."

"She buys flour and sugar in bulk." He turned onto the two-lane highway and headed toward the Andersons' property. "Back when I was in high school, she and Lucy and a handful of other Faith Trinity ladies single-handedly funded our baseball uniforms by hosting a bake sale."

"That's awesome."

"I've never seen so many pies, cakes and sweet breads

in one place. My brothers and I thought for sure we'd be eating baked goods for days. Unfortunately, the ladies sold every last one. The residents paid triple, sometimes more, for each item."

"It sounds like a lot of Cassandra Herrons live in this town."

"We like to take care of our own."

This was precisely the type of community she wanted to raise her daughter in. One where everyone seemed to know and, for the most part, get along with one another.

He turned down a long, winding dirt road, pebbles dinging his truck's undercarriage. She thought back to when she'd first ridden in his truck. She'd been so anxious, she'd about made herself sick. If he'd noticed, he hadn't mentioned anything.

He intrigued her in a way no other man, not even John, had, and she found herself wanting to know more about him. "Did you play any other sports in high school?"

"Some. Soccer for two seasons, played some football, and I ran track for a while. You?"

"I was more of a spectator, although I went to almost every game. I tried out for cheerleading once…well, sort of."

"You didn't make it?"

"I didn't stick around long enough to find out. I went to practice for maybe three weeks. Quit before auditions. I didn't like the culture."

"Oh?"

"The other girls were pretty wild. Boy-crazy partiers."

He studied her for a moment, as if her response triggered more questions, but then he focused once again on the road.

She pulled a small bottle of lotion from her purse. "Have you always wanted to be a vet?"

"Once I realized I'd never walk on the moon and was too tall to jockey." He chuckled. "Pretty much. My brothers always teased me for being too sensitive. Made jokes about how I wanted to rescue every stray or injured rabbit. Guess I've always been that way. Back when we were young—I was probably five or six at the time—my brothers did that whole salt-on-slugs thing. I got so angry, seeing those creatures writhing around. Later I learned animals with such simple nervous systems probably can't feel pain, but it still bothered me."

"Me, too."

"I sensed you have a tender heart."

"Sometimes too much."

"I don't believe a person can ever be too kind or compassionate, especially not in this field."

"Thanks." The note of admiration in his voice touched her more than it should have, and she reminded herself again that he was her boss. A boss who, for all she knew, would cut her loose as soon as her internship was over. Then she'd have no choice but to move.

Potentially, never to see him again. The notion saddened her.

Chapter Nine

Stephanie slowed as she approached a longhorn cattle ranch on her right. She glanced at the map Caden had drawn for her, then turned onto the dusty road lined with barbed wire fencing. She released a heavy breath in an attempt to calm her jitters.

"Where to, Mommy?" Maddy asked the same question she'd voiced half a dozen times since Stephanie had buckled her in.

She repeated the answer her daughter certainly had memorized by now.

"Your boss's mommy and daddy?"

"Yes, sweet girl."

"With doggies and kitties?"

"What?"

"He makes them better?"

"Oh, yes, but not tonight. There won't be any animals—well, there might be. But we're not going to the clinic."

"Where are we going?"

Sometimes Maddy seemed to remember everything, and other times, such as now, like she recalled nothing. Most likely she was just trying to connect, which was sweet. "We're going to my boss's mommy's and daddy's house for dinner."

From the sounds of it, their whole clan—Caden's three brothers and their wives and kids—would be there. A regular family reunion, with her and Maddy as the outliers. What would they talk about? Stephanie stank at surface-level conversations, especially with strangers. Or in socially awkward situations, and this little get-together was sure to involve all three.

She had half a mind to turn around and tell Caden she had a stomachache, which she was building by the mile.

She never used to feel so anxious in new situations. Her ex-husband had trained that in her. Well, it was high time she untrained it. The lies could only defeat her if she let them. He said she'd never be able to survive on her own or make anything of herself. Yet here she was, proving him wrong by steadily advancing toward her dreams.

Her mother's voice filled her thoughts. *You're a warrior. Don't ever forget that or let anyone tell you otherwise.*

She'd spoken those words the night Stephanie packed an emergency duffel bag and headed to the women and children's shelter. When what she'd really wanted to do was fly to her mom's, but she hadn't a dime to her name, nor could her mom afford to come to where she was.

She had to take that first hard step all alone. She'd felt so weak, so vulnerable and afraid. Yet exiting her house had been the bravest moment of her life. Every step after had gained momentum, until one day she packed her things once again and drove her and her sweet girl halfway across the country, not knowing for certain what lay ahead.

And once again, she'd called her mom, if only to hear her repeat what had become her favorite mantra: "You're a warrior, baby girl."

Stephanie caught her daughter's eye in the rearview mirror. "You're a warrior, sweet pea. Do you know that?"

"Wawyow?"

Laughing, she nodded. "A strong, brave, smart, beautiful and amazing warrior who can become whatever you set your mind to. Don't ever forget that or let anyone tell you otherwise."

Never, ever would she let a man hurt her daughter like John had her.

Stephanie thought of Caden's interaction with Maddy that night at the church. Standing in the doorway, Stephanie had watched them for a while. She'd studied their relaxed body language, Maddy's chirpy voice and Caden's deep yet gentle one.

What might it be like to have a family? With a loving husband who came home to dinner every night, read stories to her daughter and held Stephanie when she was sad or afraid?

She parked in the shade of a large bald cypress tree and stepped out of her vehicle, the scent of flowers, sunbaked earth and garlicky chicken wafting toward her. A sense of awe fell over her as she surveyed the colorful meadows surrounding the yellow farmhouse in every direction. The sight reminded her of something one might see in an oil painting.

Tucked within the tall grass stood boxes, sometimes stacked one on top of the other. To her left, an old-fashioned wooden windmill cast an elongated shadow across the gently swaying grass. The serenity helped soothe her nerves.

With a deep breath, she turned toward her daughter.

Still fastened in her car seat, she was frowning, fussing and tugging fiercely on her straps. "Me out, pwease!"

Laughing, Stephanie opened the back-passenger door. "Patience." Not that any three-year-old she'd ever met understood the word.

How formal would this dinner be, and how well-behaved would everyone expect Maddy to be? Hopefully she wouldn't attempt to shove peas up her nose or belt out the potty song in the middle of dinner.

The thunk of a door banging open turned her attention to the single-story yellow house to her right. Two boys, the oldest maybe aged ten, the second a year or so younger, scurried down the porch steps. They barreled past her, the younger one hollering about some injustice, and toward a faded barn at the end of a dirt road. A little girl followed, half skipping and half running.

A moment later, Caden's mom stood in the open doorway, shielding her eyes as she gazed after the children. "Those kids. Here's hoping they'll run off some of that endless energy before suppertime." She smiled, engaged Maddy in chatter for a moment, then said, "Welcome to our humble little hive."

She motioned Stephanie and Maddy into a cheery living room crowded with furniture and decorated with various bee-related knickknacks. Family pictures covered the walls, and natural light streamed in through the window, adorned with lace curtains. The laughter drifting toward them from the other room reminded Stephanie that she'd be meeting Caden's entire family tonight.

"Hi." Caden emerged wearing faded jeans, boots and a snug T-shirt that accentuated his muscular frame.

"Thanks for coming out." His gaze shifted to Maddy, and kind laughter immediately filled his eyes. "Hey. There's my buddy." He held out his hand, expecting a high five.

Maddy grinned and leaned into Stephanie.

"Come on, now." Caden palmed the air a few times. "Don't leave me hanging."

Stephanie laughed and was soon ushered into the dining room as adults and children gathered around the longest table she'd ever seen. Clanking dishes and cheerful conversation swirled around her, with everyone seamlessly interjecting into the various discussions without the slightest hint of confusion. They each had a story to tell, most of them about Caden.

"One day, he figured he'd earn his own money," his mom said. "He decided he'd take honey from the hives to do so. Learned real quick there's a right—and wrong—way to handle bees."

"Don't forget about when he went dumpster diving for old items to fix up and sell." His dad drizzled honey on his steaming roll.

Everyone laughed.

"A squirrel was hit by a car but survived," she said. "So he sneaked it home."

"He knew, and from past experience, I might add, that Mom and Dad would never let him keep it." His brother spooned more mashed potatoes on his plate.

Caden chuckled. "I was a stupid, cocky kid who thought I could save him."

His mom smiled. "A vet in the making, right, son?"

"Maybe, but I soon realized I could not play that role. That creature needed a real vet, so I called Dr. Wallow."

"He was practicing then?" Stephanie asked.

Caden nodded. "He listened patiently, then agreed to give the squirrel a look. He offered me my first real lesson on veterinary medicine, and not like someone talking to some stupid kid. He treated me like an intelligent adult capable of handling tough decisions. He also told me the squirrel would die without surgery, which I obviously didn't have the money for. But I thought maybe I could paint up an old dresser or bookshelf and sell it at the antiques store to cover the costs."

"He filled our garage with all sorts of junk." Caden's dad poured more sweet tea into his glass.

Stephanie's phone vibrated in her back pocket, and she pulled it out to look at the screen. Rhonda Chandler, the director of the Next Steps program. She also supervised the

Get ready to relax and indulge with your **FREE BOOKS** and more!

**Claim up to FOUR NEW BOOKS & TWO MYSTERY GIFTS –
absolutely FREE!**

Dear Reader,

We both know life can be difficult at times. That's why it's important to treat yourself so you can relax and recharge once in a while.

And I'd like to help you do this by sending you this amazing offer of up to FOUR brand new full length FREE BOOKS that WE pay for.

This is everything I have ready to send to you right now:

Try **Love Inspired® Romance Larger-Print** books and fall in love with inspirational romances that take you on an uplifting journey of faith, forgiveness and hope.

Try **Love Inspired® Suspense Larger-Print** books where courage and optimism unite in stories of faith and love in the face of danger.

Or TRY BOTH!

All we ask in return is that you answer 4 simple questions on the attached Treat Yourself survey. You'll get **Two Free Books** and **Two Mystery Gifts** from each series you try, *altogether worth over $20!* Who could pass up a deal like that?

Sincerely,

Pam Powers

Harlequin Reader Service

Treat Yourself to Free Books and Free Gifts.

Answer 4 fun questions and get rewarded.

	YES	NO
1. I LOVE reading a good book.	◯	◯
2. I indulge and "treat" myself often.	◯	◯
3. I love getting FREE things.	◯	◯
4. Reading is one of my favorite activities.	◯	◯

▶ DETACH AND MAIL CARD TODAY!

TREAT YOURSELF • Pick your 2 Free Books...

Yes! Please send me my Free Books from each series I select and Free Mystery Gifts. I understand that I am under no obligation to buy anything, as explained on the back of this card.

Which do you prefer?
- ❏ **Love Inspired® Romance Larger-Print** 122/322 IDL GRDP
- ❏ **Love Inspired® Suspense Larger-Print** 107/307 IDL GRDP
- ❏ **Try Both** 122/322 & 107/307 IDL GRED

FIRST NAME   LAST NAME

ADDRESS

APT.#   CITY

STATE/PROV.   ZIP/POSTAL CODE

EMAIL ❏   Please check this box if you would like to receive newsletters and promotional emails from Harlequin Enterprises ULC and its affiliates. You can unsubscribe anytime.

© 2022 HARLEQUIN ENTERPRISES ULC
™ and ® are trademarks owned by Harlequin Enterprises ULC. Printed in the U.S.A.

LI/SLI-520-TY22

▲ If offer card is missing write to: Harlequin Reader Service, P.O. Box 1341, Buffalo, NY 14240-8531 or visit www.ReaderService.com ▲

BUSINESS REPLY MAIL
FIRST-CLASS MAIL PERMIT NO. 717 BUFFALO, NY

POSTAGE WILL BE PAID BY ADDRESSEE

HARLEQUIN READER SERVICE
PO BOX 1341
BUFFALO NY 14240-8571

NO POSTAGE
NECESSARY
IF MAILED
IN THE
UNITED STATES

women and children's shelter where Stephanie and Maddy had stayed.

Why would she be calling? Had something happened?

"Everything alright?" Mrs. Stoughton studied her with a furrowed brow.

"Yes, ma'am. What were you saying?"

"They were just sharing more embarrassing stories about me." Caden placed his wadded napkin on his plate. "As if you need to hear more."

His mom stood and began gathering empty dishes. "Why don't you give her a tour of the property, dear?" She turned to Stephanie. "Have you ever been to a bee farm?"

She chewed her bottom lip as an image of her little one swarmed with bees gripped her mind. She didn't want to seem overly fearful, especially considering Caden held the power to hire her or let her go. But bees and Maddy...

"Don't worry." Caden smiled. "The critters have probably hunkered down for the night. Even so, we'll stay well enough away from them. Not that they'd bother you any. So long as folks leave them alone, they tend to do the same. We might as well stop by to see the horses, too."

"Howsies?" Maddy lifted big, hopeful eyes to Stephanie.

She couldn't help but share her enthusiasm. You'd think, being a vet tech, her awe of horses would go away. If anything, she'd only grown to love them more. They had such a sweetness about them, with their ability to sense a person's feelings. "Maddy would love that."

The other children clamored from their chairs, asking nearly in unison, "Us, too?"

Mrs. Stoughton shook her head. "Y'all get plenty of riding time. Tonight you get to act like gracious hosts and give our guests a turn."

They moaned and sagged so melodramatically they elicited laughter in the adults.

"But you can go feed the chickens."

Apparently they didn't find this a decent trade. One of them crossed her arms with an exaggerated pout. Another released the loudest, most animated sigh possible. And another started whining about how unfair their grandmother was being.

"Come on, now." Mr. Stoughton ruffled the complaining boy's hair. "You can do better than that. You've got to put your whole torso in it, like this." He mimicked the child and flopped forward.

At first, the kid appeared irritated, but after a few more imitations, punctuated by his PopPop's playful pokes to the ribs, he started giggling.

"Now go find some chickens to pester." He sent the child off with a wink and a gentle nudge that Stephanie certainly hadn't anticipated when she'd first walked in. Based on the man's size and gruff, weathered appearance, she'd expected him to be surly. Maybe even angry.

But his eyes radiated the same humor and kindness she always saw in Caden's.

The same gentleness she saw in all the Stoughton men, even the louder and more boisterous ones. And the women clearly felt relaxed as everyone teased one another.

Like she used to see in a TV sitcom she once watched, back when she'd felt like a prisoner in her own home. She used to fantasize what it felt like to live in such a family.

She'd imagined it something like this.

Caden led Stephanie and her daughter down the porch steps to one of three paved paths he, his brothers and father created decades ago. One direction led to the horse pasture and stables, another to their display hives for when school groups came out and the third to a gazebo set in a small rock garden.

Eyeing the sinking sun, he debated where to take her and Maddy first. If only he had more time, though there was no reason he couldn't ask her out here again. As a friend, of course. Because despite his physical attraction, and even growing respect and admiration, he couldn't let himself fall for her. He'd help her as he could, yes, as was his duty as her boss and a Christian, but no more.

Unless... He knew of some vets who successfully worked with their spouses, but he was pretty sure they'd all been married first. Still, she did fit well at the clinic. Here among his family, as well.

Thankfully, his siblings hadn't grilled her on her past or her staying with the Herrons.

But their immediate concern had exacerbated one of his. How would her background and any assumptions regarding it hinder client trust? Trust that was already somewhat shaky with Dr. Wallow gone.

An equally important question: Could he trust her?

He thought again of his medicine inventory and the spike in his order. Surely that had nothing to do with Stephanie. Even if she had the inclination, he couldn't imagine she'd be so brazen, so soon into her internship. Although he knew drugs could cause people to do foolish things.

He'd heard stories about vet techs stealing drugs and had even taken continuing education workshops on issues related to the ongoing opioid crisis. But surely he would've noticed signs of drug use, and she didn't seem the stealing type.

No. Though she could be a little jumpy, she had kind and honest eyes. And she seemed like such a great, attentive mother, one who'd never endanger her daughter in such a way.

There had to be another explanation.

He cast her a sideways glance. She gazed out across the breeze-stirred meadow, as if lost in the beauty of her surroundings. But what drew him to her most was her patience with Maddy as she peppered her with one question

after another, often before Stephanie had a chance to answer the previous.

She'd been equally gracious with his nieces and nephews. Her responses indicated more than tolerance. She actually seemed to enjoy them.

"Mama, look! A poly-poly." Maddy squatted down and
pinched a pill bug between her fingers.

Stephanie lowered to her level with a warm smile reflected in her soft blue eyes. "I see."

"I keep it?"

She laughed. "Wouldn't that be fun? But this is his
home."

"He move."

"What about his family? His mommy and daddy and
sisters and brothers? They'd want him to stay."

"And their nanna?"

Sadness shadowed her previously joyful expression.
"And their nanna, yes."

Once again, he wondered about her past, not just what
had brought her here, but what all she might've left behind.

Maddy stared at the insect a moment more, before re-
leasing it and turning toward a cluster of black-eyed Susans.
Plopping on her rear, she began tugging at the flowers, their
blossoms popping off while their roots remained intact.

"Are you and your mom close?" Caden plucked a long
piece of straw.

Stephanie nodded.

"You must miss her."

"I do. Thankfully, there's always FaceTime. Unfortunately, Maddy isn't a fan of talking to a screen. But on
occasion, especially when she's tired, she'll listen quietly
while my mom reads one of her favorite stories. Of course,
it helps when my mom uses different voices."

"What a great way to stay connected."

Her smile returned. "That's sort of my mom's thing.

She was a single parent and worked long hours, sometimes holding down two jobs. But she always tried to tuck me in at night and read me stories. My favorite has become Maddy's as well—*Kay-Kay and the Runaway Berry*. It's about a little girl who plants berry seeds. They grow into a vine that eventually produces a plump berry. The berry comes alive and runs away, dancing and skipping along the countryside, engaging in all sorts of hilarious, unexpected adventures."

An image surfaced of Stephanie holding Maddy close. The soft glow of the evening light shimmering off her silky black hair, similar to how the setting sun caressed her now. Her long lashes brushing against her cheeks as she gazed lovingly at her daughter.

Maddy's shrill giggle interrupted his thoughts. She scampered ahead, chasing after a dragonfly.

He couldn't help but laugh at her pure delight. "If only we could bottle up some of that joy, huh?"

"I agree."

They continued to the old cedar elm with the tire swing he and his brothers swung on for so many summers, the one his nieces and nephews still enjoyed. "Would she like to swing for a spell?"

Stephanie's eyes lit up. "She'd love that. Thanks for thinking of her." She called her daughter over and lifted her onto the tire. Then she stepped back and allowed him to push Maddy while she watched with a hint of a smile.

He was surprised by how comfortable this felt, the three of them together. Surprised he didn't feel the need to fill moments of silence or say something witty. And if Stephanie's relaxed demeanor was any indication, she felt similar.

This was so much different than the last couple of dates he'd gone on, one where the woman had talked nonstop, and mainly about herself. During the second, the conversation had felt so stilted. Then there'd been Renée.

Her betrayal had done more than break his heart. It'd messed with his mind and his ability to trust.

But it was time he quit giving that past hurt such a strong hold on him.

Every woman he met wasn't a Renée.

Once Maddy lost interest with the swing, they continued to the gazebo where she soon occupied herself with smooth rocks she pretended were people or baby dolls.

"This is so beautiful." Stephanie gazed at the wooden structure, partially covered in flowering vines.

"My brothers and I helped my dad build it years ago."

Green bushes bordered its base. Behind it stretched a sea of color created by the countless wildflowers bursting through the grassland, providing ample pollen for the bees.

Stephanie tucked a lock of hair behind her ear. "Did you guys come out here often when you were growing up?"

"At first. My mom would pack lunch or dinner in a picnic basket and we'd all come here to eat. Eventually, my brothers and I grew tired of that, so she only brought us out once or twice a summer. But she and Dad spent a lot of time out here. Still do, actually, sipping on fresh-squeezed lemonade and staring up at the moon and stars."

"That sounds so romantic."

It did, evoking images of him and Stephanie sitting in the gazebo, his arm around her shoulder, her head resting on his chest.

Reining in his thoughts, he cleared his throat. "We should probably head to the stables before it gets too late."

"That'd be awesome. Thank you. I mean that." Tears pooled in her eyes. "Thank you for being so kind. To both of us."

The way she looked at him stalled his breath. "No problem."

He sensed they were treading close to something Stephanie might not be ready for, something that maybe wouldn't even be fair to her. If they started dating, would she feel tied to the clinic? When she needed the freedom to explore every career option. Not to mention, there was Maddy to consider.

If they did date, he needed to make sure he was ready for a romantic relationship *and* fatherhood, and that meant more than simply sitting at the dinner table every once in a while. Maddy deserved someone who would truly be there for her.

But he'd learned the hard way, just because he was all in didn't mean there wouldn't be heartache. His failure to think things through had hurt a kid once. He refused to repeat his mistake with Maddy.

As they neared the stables, his nephew came bounding toward him, cheeks red. "Uncle Caden? Dessert's ready. Mama said I could come get you now."

He laughed. "Why do I get the feeling you kids pestered your grandparents nonstop since Ms. Stephanie and I stepped outside? Acting like custard would up and slide away if you don't devour it immediately."

His nephew stared back at him with such an innocent expression Caden could barely keep a straight face.

"Sorry, bud." Caden rustled his hair. "But I haven't given these ladies that horse ride I promised them."

"Can't they come back another time?"

"That wouldn't be very mannerly of me, now would it?"

His nephew lowered his head. "No, sir."

"It's okay." Stephanie touched Caden's arm, her skin buttery smooth. "Another time would probably be best. I should get this little one to bed soon." She grazed the side of Maddy's face with the back of her hand.

"Yeah, sure."

Another time.

With the woman who was quickly invading his thoughts despite his efforts to the contrary.

What might happen if he quit fighting his feelings?

His brain told him that would be reckless, but his heart wasn't listening.

Chapter Ten

T he next morning, Stephanie hustled to work, anxious to check her voice mail from the night before. Her phone must've fallen out of her pocket during her tour of Caden's property. She hadn't realized this until she'd gotten into her car. While she'd wanted to go search for it, by then Maddy had been well past her limit.

Thankfully, Caden had offered to find it and bring it to the clinic.

Hopefully, he had. They'd crossed a lot of ground.

What a lovely evening they'd had! Phone loss and all, she was glad she chose not to back out. She was tempted to believe Caden enjoyed their time together just as much.

Was she fooling herself to think that maybe something could develop between them? He was her boss. Obviously, the boss-employee relationship could complicate things.

And if she worked elsewhere, perhaps with the mobile vet?

With all the animosity Caden seemed to hold for Dr. Elkins, something told her that would be a bad idea.

Was she really evaluating job options based on her feelings for Caden? And if so, was that wrong? After all, this situation was nothing like what she'd experienced with John.

Smiling, she reflected on the laughter and conversation that had swirled around the Stoughtons' dinner table. It reminded her of when she'd joined her third-grade best friend for her family's Fourth of July celebrations out on her grandparents' farm. There'd been so many people, so much food and so much joy.

While she adored her mom, having been an only child raised by a single parent who often needed two jobs to pay the bills, many times Stephanie's home had felt too quiet. Lonely.

She doubted any of the Stoughton kids had ever felt that way.

Her heart warmed as she thought of how sweet Caden had been with Maddy—pushing her on the swing, listening to her chatter about flowers and bugs as if her every word were the most fascinating thing he'd heard all evening.

He'd make a good father.

Why wasn't he one already, or at least married? Because of his job?

Probably. With how many hours he worked, the man clearly didn't have time for much else.

Common sense told her to resist her growing attraction.

Only her feelings were more than that. Much more.

She checked her reflection in her rearview mirror, grabbed her things and stepped out of her vehicle. The early-morning air still held that fresh, after-a-midnight-rain scent.

She paused. Her phone! Had it remained outside and gotten drenched? If so, it'd be ruined, and a new one would practically eat her entire paycheck. That wouldn't be a huge deal, considering she had so few bills, if she knew the Herrons would let her stay longer and she had a full-time job waiting.

She sighed and scanned the parking lot.

Apparently Lisa was late this morning. Odd. Assuming

the front doors hadn't been unlocked, she entered through the back.

"Lisa, is that you?" Caden's voice drifted down the hall and broke through her mental wrestling.

"No. Stephanie."

"Oh."

He sounded disappointed. Had she misinterpreted their evening together? Those moments when it'd seemed as if he hadn't wanted to be anywhere else or with anyone else?

Maybe that was for the best. She wasn't sure his work habits would be the best fit. If she ever did remarry, she wanted the full package—a man who loved her *and* would be the type of father Maddy needed. Granted, as a vet tech, her schedule would be busy as well, but she'd guard her off-days and prioritize time with Maddy.

Whomever she became involved with needed to do the same.

But all her logic didn't stop her from primping her hair as she walked down the hall to his office. She poked her head inside. "Hi."

He sat behind his desk, and the clutter spilled before him seemed to have increased significantly. "Hey. Did Maddy make it home before crashing?"

She smiled. "Barely."

"I could tell she was wiped with the way she kept rubbing her eyes."

"She sure had fun, and this morning, she talked about the 'horsies' almost nonstop. She wanted to know their names, where their mommies and daddies were."

He chuckled. "That peanut is something else."

"Her brain cracks me up, how quickly she can grow a fantasy into a reality. My mom says she's going to be a novelist one day."

She surveyed the opened files and papers spread before them, and wondered once again about the clinic's finances.

For Caden's sake as much as her own. The poor man didn't need another loss.

Not to mention, she needed to cut him some slack when his greeting or tone didn't match her expectations. The man was obviously doing all he could to keep things together.

But that brought her back to her doubts regarding his emotional availability.

"Did you manage to find my phone?"

He glanced up. "Huh? Oh, right." He pulled it from his vet bag and handed it over. "Want to guess where it was?"

"At the gazebo?"

"Nope. In the pantry, of all places."

"What? Really?" She hadn't gone close to the pantry.

"Yep. One of the kids must've found it. Hopefully they didn't call China."

She laughed. "No worries. I password-protected it the moment Maddy started turning random items from my purse into her personal playthings."

He smiled. "I remember when my nieces and nephews went through that phase." He paused. "Guess they haven't left it just yet, huh?"

"Guess not."

Uneasiness settled in her gut as she once again thought of why the shelter's Next Steps director might be calling her. But unfortunately, her phone was dead.

Why did she always fear the worst? For all Stephanie knew, she wanted to talk to her about her stay with the Herrons or how her internship was going.

"Everything okay?" Caden studied her with a concerned look.

"Absolutely. You wouldn't happen to have a charger, would you?"

"Sure." He scrounged around in his desk until he produced a neon-green cord.

"Hey, all!" Lisa's voice emanated from the lobby, as

loud as ever. "Thought I was going to be late. Got stuck behind a train on the other side of East Elm." She kept talking, but Stephanie was too focused on her phone to pay much attention.

Unfortunately, the rest of morning was so busy she wasn't able to check her voice mail until lunch.

Then, with a deep breath, she grabbed her phone and played the message. "Hi, Stephanie. This is Rhonda Chandler from the Fresh Hope Women and Children's Shelter. Can you please return my call at your earliest convenience?"

She glanced at the time on her screen. Hopefully Rhonda wasn't in a meeting or leading a Next Steps class.

She hit the dial icon, pleasantly surprised when Rhonda answered.

"Stephanie, thank you for calling me back so quickly."

"Of course. Is everything alright?"

"Oh, I'm sure it is, but we like to be cautious when it comes to you ladies."

Her hands felt cold. "About?"

"Someone broke into our main office over the weekend, ransacked our things and got into our safe. We suspect one of our former residents whom we had to ask to leave, due to noncompliance. However, well, I'm sure you can understand our concern."

Stephanie felt like the air had been squeezed out of her lungs. If the shelter's name and location got out, if their records got out, they would all be at risk. And what if the intruder hadn't been the woman Rhonda expected? What if it was someone's former abuser, maybe even John?

No. She was being paranoid. There was no way he could know she'd gone to that shelter. Was there? She tried to remember if she'd ever mentioned her stay to anyone that he might come into contact with. Or if any of the women she met there had exes in prison or who had been in prison.

Her churning stomach was overreacting. Again. But she'd lived on hyperalert for so long, sometimes her body responded on its own accord. Like now.

She closed her eyes and practiced one of the deep-breathing exercises her former therapist had taught her. In through the nose. Out through the mouth.

"Stephanie?"

She glanced up to see Caden standing in the break room doorway, watching her. "Is everything al right?"

Stephanie forced a smile, wishing she didn't feel so jittery. She hated that her ex-husband still had such a hold on her.

"I'm great." Squaring her shoulders, she slipped her phone into the pocket of her scrubs top. "Did you need something?"

The worry lines stretching across Caden's brow suggested he didn't believe her. While touched by his obvious concern, she'd much rather trigger his confidence.

Caden watched Stephanie escort a client from an exam room to the lobby. She seemed okay, even cheerful now, but whomever she'd called had really shaken her up. Why?

He'd say it wasn't any of his business, but he was worried—about her and his business. He found himself questioning everything and everyone, and he hated that. He'd never been the suspicious type.

Losing a large amount of narcotics had changed that. Until he had answers regarding the missing medications, he had to remain alert to *everything*. Changes of behavior, people acting nervous, secretive.

His heart told him Stephanie wasn't to blame and stirred him to rise to her defense. But he'd learned his lesson with Renée not to let his emotions—and a pretty smile—dominate and override his logic.

His phone rang. A local number that looked familiar. He swallowed a bite of his tuna sandwich. "Dr. Stoughton."

"Yes, hello." The soft, almost gravelly reply reminded him of his grandmother's voice. "This is Maybelle, Lola's mom."

Lola. He sifted through patient names, trying unsuccessfully to recall what animal the woman was referring to. "Yes, ma'am. How can I help you?"

"My sweet girl is healthy as a fiddle, thank goodness, so you don't have to worry none about her. But, well, I thought you should know, Renée stopped by this morning to check on my fur baby. Did you know she moved back to town?"

A tendon in his jaw twitched. "Yes, ma'am."

"Apparently she's opened a mobile vet or some such thing and wanted to tell me about her great rates. No offense, but they're much lower than what y'all charge."

Lisa had been right. Renée was actively trying to steal his clients, and based on this phone call, her efforts were proving effective. "Okay." He rubbed his forehead, waiting for Maybelle to politely cut ties with the clinic.

"I've been coming to y'all since Lola was a pup, and I don't see any reason to switch now. But, well, I'm not so sure my neighbors will say the same."

"Ma'am?"

"Renée's been talking to a lot of folks, handing out flyers and whatnot. I'm pretty sure everyone around here takes their pets to see you. None of us have seen any reason to drive to that fancy clinic some fifteen minutes away when we can get proper care from you. But, well, with Dr. Wallow gone…"

He feared even those loyal enough to stay would probably want a discount. Especially if Renée was out there proclaiming unrealistically low fees. How could she afford that? Then again, she didn't have a building to maintain and air-condition or a staff to support.

Something clients wouldn't understand or likely even take the time to consider.

"I appreciate you letting me know." He tensed, waiting for the price reduction he worried she was about to request.

"I worry other folks might not be so loyal, especially those who were partial to Renée. I just thought you should know, is all."

That anyone could feel partial to that lying, conniving woman baffled him. Then again, she'd fooled him—and Dr. Wallow. Though he blamed himself for the latter. Wallow never would've hired Renée if not for Caden.

"I appreciate the call." And he did, even if he couldn't do anything about it. He certainly couldn't lower his prices. Nor would he allow his ex to have such sway over his decisions. He'd simply have to trust God to act as judge, provider and defender.

He'd just hung up when Lisa tapped on his open door. "There's a Dr. Jones to see you."

"Walk him back, please."

Lisa nodded and disappeared, her rubber shoes squeaking on the linoleum. He reviewed the documents the agency had sent him. The man seemed to cover a relatively large area. While that would limit his availability, he came highly recommended.

The squeak of Lisa's shoes returned, grew louder, then stopped. She and a thin, balding man with a large Adam's apple appeared in his doorway.

Caden crossed the room to greet him. "Hello, thank you for coming." He shook Dr. Jones's hand, surprised by his weak grip. "Please, have a seat." He motioned toward the folding chair positioned in front of his desk and winced at the overall lack of professionalism his office must've conveyed.

Though he'd tidied his desk, boxes of files he was still trying to make sense of lined the walls. Or rather, boxes of files he was using to try to make sense of the last few months' worth of records and numbers. The yellow metal filing cabinet that was probably older than the worn and stained carpet. Their desks, both purchased at local garage sales, though at different times, separated by a long stretch of black rug decorated in paw prints and dog-related puns.

"Can I get you something? Coffee or water?" Caden asked.

"No, but thank you."

With a nod, Caden returned to his desk. "So, tell me, what motivated you to go into vet relief work?"

The man shrugged. "I love animals, obviously, and knew I wanted a career in veterinary medicine. But I wanted to travel the country while I was still able. I have no doubt I'll settle down eventually, maybe start my own practice in a small ranching community like this one, but for now, I enjoy the flexibility and freedom my position allows."

Caden's attention perked up. Based on the slight dusting of gray at his temples, his crow's feet and the fine lines stretched across his forehead, he was in his mid to late thirties. His days of living in transit would probably end soon enough. However, it was just as likely he'd hire on with a clinic elsewhere, one whose finances weren't so tight. Or, like he said, start his own practice.

Caden read over his information again, including his desired pay. "How many days a month would you be available?"

"I plan to spend the summer in Boerne, so I could easily pop over once a week."

"Do you have family there?"

"My grandparents—twenty minutes from here." The man frowned. "My grandfather has prostate cancer, and my grandmother needs help caring for him, getting him to his appointments and whatnot."

"I'm sorry to hear that." Although that was good news

for him. Once a week would be a huge help, especially since his sheet indicated he preferred working weekends.

"Thanks."

They talked a while longer—about what type of personal equipment and liability insurance he had, what cases he felt comfortable handling, and about Sage Creek culture. "Our older clients might have a difficult time seeing someone they don't know." And an out-of-towner on top of that. "They were partial to Dr. Wallow."

"I understand."

"'Course people can surprise you." He closed Dr. Jones's file and pushed away from his desk. "I'll get back to you by mid next week."

The man stood, and Caden walked him out, nodding to clients in the lobby as he passed. He paused at the clinic entrance to thank the man once more, then meandered back to the reception desk. Lisa was talking with a pet owner who'd been in a few days before. Her dog, an older German Shepherd–husky mix who used to see Dr. Wallow, lay at her feet with his muzzle resting on his paw.

He'd developed osteoarthritis, and it had progressed to the point where anti-inflammatories were no longer working. Wallow had placed the dog on tramadol. Caden had provided a refill mere days before.

Why was she here now? He squatted down to scratch Rufus behind his ears. "Hey, boy. Did you miss us?" The dog lifted his beautiful big eyes to meet Caden's, but otherwise remained lying on the linoleum. Caden stood and faced his owner with a smile. "Hello, ma'am. Is everything alright?"

"My Rufus seems to be in more pain, more than normal. He's reluctant to go outside, and when I tried to take him for a walk, we barely made it to the end of the drive before he just laid down and wouldn't move. And he struggles to get up, especially first thing in the morning or after taking a nap."

"You're giving him tramadol?"

She nodded. "But I'm not sure it's still working."

"Is it possible he's injured?" It wasn't uncommon for dogs to get hit by cars without their owners knowing.

"He never goes out unless I take him."

"Could he have stumbled down stairs or anything?"

"I live in a mobile home."

"Bring him back and I'll—" The numbers from Stephanie's inventory, which Lisa had verified, came to mind. "Do you have his medication with you, by chance?"

She nodded and dug through her purse. "I wasn't sure if you'd want it back—if you could swap it out for something different. Something stronger, maybe." She handed over the pill bottle.

He verified the drug name on the label, then he opened the bottle and peered inside. The pills were small, white and oval, and had *4H2* printed on them. Odd. He poured a few in his hand. "Is there any chance you got medications mixed up?"

"What do you mean?"

"Did you pour any out, to put in a pill tray or anything, and possibly return them to the wrong bottle?"

"No."

"Can you excuse me a moment?"

"Yes, of course."

He hurried to where he kept the narcotics, opened the safe and grabbed one of the tramadol bottles. The pills inside looked the same as those from his client. He put that bottle back and grabbed the next one. The pills inside were round, like he'd expect. He poured a couple in his hand and read their inscription. *DRA?* He tried the next bottle. Those pills were labeled *58*.

His stomach soured. This wasn't right. He dashed into

his office and typed the first inscription into his search engine. He blinked. Allergy medication? He typed it in again with the same results. He tried the inscription on the pills in the next bottle. A brand name for dimenhydrinate, which treated dizziness.

Someone was messing with the medications. His mind spun as he considered the possible fallout. Patients given who knows what. He could be sued. Worse, what if someone turned him in to the DEA? He could lose his license.

There was no way this was an accident. But stuff like this, people stealing medication, happened at other clinics. Not here. He knew and trusted his staff. They'd never had problems before.

Not until Dr. Wallow's death.

And Stephanie's arrival.

His heart sank. Surely she wasn't doing drugs. She didn't seem the type. She was too gentle, well-mannered and kind. Too…

Beautiful? Was he blinded by her sweet demeanor and innocent looks? This wouldn't be the first time he'd fallen for a woman who wasn't anything like he'd thought.

Chapter Eleven

Stephanie paused in the hall to release a heavy breath. This morning had been more challenging than normal. One pet owner had refused to believe her dog had cancer and accused Caden of diagnosing diseases with the most expensive treatment plans. Their next client complained of the opposite. When she learned of her cat's terminal prognosis, she told the entire office how her Chester deserved a vet who'd "fight for him."

While Caden handled each instance with calm grace, Stephanie could tell the increased tension wore on him.

Thankfully, the dog owner duo who occupied their last appointment before lunch was rather endearing. The man's throaty laugh and cheesy jokes lightened the atmosphere, although Caden still appeared tense. Anxious and almost suspicious. More than once, Stephanie caught him watching her with a strange expression.

Similar to how her ex-husband used to scrutinize her when he thought she'd been up to something. The man had barely allowed her to leave the house.

Was Caden the jealous type? Did he have a temper? If so, would she have seen it by now?

She recalled his interaction with a frightened dachshund who'd tried to bite him numerous times. Not once had

Caden appeared even slightly agitated. No. She was being ridiculous. He was perhaps the gentlest man she'd ever met.

So why was he acting so strange? Had she done something? Upset a client in some way? If so, surely he would've addressed her directly.

Though he might've lacked time. Amid their rather hectic morning, he'd managed to interview three potential vets. Based on his facial expressions after each, he hadn't been impressed with the first two applicants. As to the third, she wasn't sure.

How long could he continue managing this clinic on his own?

The front door whooshed open, and a scowling woman with frizzy blond hair puffing out from a glittery pink visor entered and marched to the counter.

"Hello." Lisa's smile appeared leery. "May I help you?"

The woman glared at Caden. "You should be ashamed of yourself, charging so much. All because folks have no other options, unless they want to drive hither and yon."

"I'm sorry you feel that way, Mrs. . . . ?"

"See? You don't even remember my name."

Caden seemed to struggle for words. But then with a visibly deep breath, his easy, and usually calming, smile reappeared. "Is there a particular charge or procedure you're concerned about?"

"All of them."

"Excuse me?"

"All your fees are ridiculous. But how were people like me supposed to know any better? I'm sure that's what you were banking on—that we'd blindly keep paying double for what things should cost. Oh, but we know now, thanks to that sweet lady running that vet-in-a-van, or whatever she calls it."

A tendon in Caden's jaw twitched. "I can understand your confusion." His gaze flickered to the lobby where a few other clients with pets gawked. Likely wondering if there was any validity to what the woman said.

He kept his smile in place. "But I'm sure you can—"

"Oh, I ain't confused. Nor do I need any sweet-talking from you or your greedy staff. Just give me my Ralph's medical records so I can take my business where I won't be gouged. Capitalizing on folks' tender hearts and love for their pets. Like I said, you should be ashamed of yourself."

Lisa snorted. "You're the one who should be ashamed, storming in here like some crazy woman."

"Lisa." Caden placed a hand on her arm. "Please make copies of Mrs.…"

"Robertson. Marianne Robertson. And I want the originals."

"Unfortunately, by law, I need those for my records. But Lisa will be more than happy to get you copies."

Lisa huffed and stood.

Meanwhile, the woman used her time waiting to address everyone in the lobby, touting how much they'd save if they went to see her Ralph's new doctor, who was "just precious and oh so kind."

Stephanie resisted the urge to roll her eyes and called back their next patient, a three-legged cat who, according to her records, Dr. Wallow had performed an amputation on about four months prior. Caden joined them shortly after she'd finished her preliminary questions. Thankfully, the rest of the exam and the three that followed went well.

Still, the tension she'd sensed when she'd walked in that morning only heightened, making her feel frazzled and insecure. Certainly not confident enough to discuss her future employment, as she'd hoped to do. She'd sent out numerous résumés and wanted to know where she stood with Caden before taking time off for interviews.

But she refused to cower to insecurity. Like her mother

had said a hundred times, she was a strong, courageous woman who pursued her dreams with determination.

While Stephanie didn't always feel the statement, she knew bravery didn't increase through avoidance.

She poked her head into Caden's office. Back to her, he was riffling through one of numerous boxes lining the far wall.

She rapped on the opened door.

He glanced over his shoulder, then turned face her. "Hey."

"You have a minute?"

"Sure." He studied her, then took a seat behind his desk. "You okay?"

"Yes, thank you." She sat in the folding chair across from him. "I was just, well, I wanted to talk about my position here."

"You're unhappy with your internship?" The cautious glint she'd seen in his eyes earlier reappeared. Not a good sign.

"Not at all. I've learned so much, and I've especially appreciated the opportunity to shadow you in the field."

"Okay. Then what seems to be the problem?"

"I'll need to find employment, once my internship ends. And well, I was wondering…"

"If there's a future for you here?"

She nodded.

He leaned forward, resting on his elbows. "You're great with the patients, and you have a way with the little dogs especially. My primary focus, however, is to find an additional vet. As to whether or not I'll hire someone to fill a tech position…" His brow pinched. "I imagine Dr. Wallow did a background check on you when you applied?"

"I think so."

"Unfortunately, I can't find those records, and I'm trying to make sure we've got all our ducks in a row. I'm sure you can understand."

"Of course."

"Would you mind consenting to another?"

Did that mean he was considering her for a long-term position? She hid her grin behind what she hoped to be a more professional but equally warm smile. "Absolutely."

"Great." He slid a form across his desk and handed her a pen.

As she signed her name, her smile grew. Why would he go through the trouble and expense if he wasn't strongly considering keeping her on? The thought sent a flutter through her midsection, and not just because of the job.

She started to scold herself for her feelings, but then stopped. Maybe it was time she quit living scared, time she released her death grip on her heart.

Maybe, just maybe, she was ready to date again.

What if her dreams of finding her happily-ever-after weren't dead after all?

Rocky, a small bichon–mixed breed abandoned at the clinic, greeted Caden when he pulled onto the long gravel road leading to his house.

He slowed to a stop and opened his door. "Come on in."

Rocky jumped onto his lap and immediately started licking Caden's face. "Alright, now. That's enough." He ran a hand down his fluffy white fur and positioned him on the seat beside him. "You act like you haven't seen me in months."

Then again, he'd been pretty busy. His dogs had every right to feel neglected. Thankfully, his neighbor popped by periodically to give both dogs love and treats. Considering they had plenty of shade, water and free range, that was all they needed. In return, Caden provided the neighbor with occasional equine care.

Hopefully, once Dr. Jones came on staff next week, Caden's stress and workload would lessen considerably and he'd have more time to spend at home.

Relaxing on his porch with an iced glass of sweet tea, with nothing to do but listen to the crickets chirp.

Gravel pinged his truck's undercarriage as he neared his house. The trees lining the road cast elongated shadows onto the landscape, and storm clouds advanced across the darkening sky. The weatherman predicted heavy rain and strong winds. Would that mess with Rheanna's barn dance fundraiser on Saturday?

She might cancel.

Then he wouldn't see Stephanie. Wouldn't have the chance to dance with her. To hold her close and breathe in the sweet scent of her shampoo.

He parked and shook his head. He couldn't be thinking that way. His attraction toward her would only cloud his judgment, and he needed to remain sharp now more than ever.

Could she have stolen meds from the clinic? She didn't seem the type. Truth was, he didn't want her to be, a fact that made him less than unbiased.

Was that why he'd been trying so hard to find a logical reason for the spike in medicine usage? He must've gone over his records half a dozen times, hoping he'd find some logical explanation. But he couldn't deny the evidence any longer. Someone had stolen clinic narcotics, and as much as he hated to admit it, as of now, Stephanie seemed the most likely culprit.

He knew nothing of her past. And while she seemed responsible enough, the fact that she was living with the Herrons left cause for concern. Still, it wasn't fair to hang all his suspicions on her.

Lisa had been territorial, snarky, but she'd acted like that for as long as he'd known her. Then again, he didn't know how long all this had been going on. Maybe someone had been stealing medications for some time and had grown bolder, cockier or sloppy. Not to mention, Lisa had seemed determined to block Stephanie from the inventory, and she had the code to their locked medications.

Then there was the little notebook of passwords and such Wallow had kept hidden deep in his desk. Who all knew about that? He tried to remember who'd wandered in and out of the office. Pretty much their whole staff at some point, as well as Wallow's family and Caden's mom. Jeff had brought his schoolbooks on numerous occasions. Said he studied better at the clinic than at home with all his siblings pestering him.

The theft was largely Caden's fault. He and Wallow had been too lax, too trusting. And now he needed to figure out proper reporting protocol.

He opened his door, waited for Rocky to jump out, then grabbed his computer bag filled with papers from the clinic. As he stepped out, Rocky danced around his feet, looking to play. Caden picked up a stick and tossed it as far as he could. Rocky bolted after it but got distracted by a squirrel halfway there.

Oh, to be so carefree.

Caden really needed more time off. Then again, if he didn't figure out what was going on at the clinic, he'd soon have more time on his hands than he'd ever wanted.

He would *not* tank the business.

And if this medicine mess cost him his license? With a sigh, he turned toward his house.

Bella, Caden's black Lab mix, lay on the porch, with her graying muzzle on stretched-out paws. The dog raised her head as Caden approached and lifted droopy eyes in greeting. Caden paused to give her a pet, then lumbered inside to make himself a pot of coffee. What he really needed was a solid eight hours of sleep.

He picked up his phone and dialed. Sheriff Alfred Talbert, a longtime family friend, answered. Caden explained the situation.

"You sure?" The man's drawl was as thick as ever.

"I wish I could think of some other explanation." What if people suspected him? He could exonerate himself with a drug test easily enough, but what would all this do to client trust? Trust that was already shaky.

"Alright. You at the clinic now?"

"No. Need me to head back?"

"Affirmative. But give me about thirty minutes to finish something up here at the station. You'll want to report this to the DEA."

"Yeah." Kneading his temple, Caden thanked him and hung up to eat a bite, give his dogs their supper and head back out.

His mom called him halfway to the clinic. When he answered, his voice must've carried some of the weariness he felt, because she asked him what was wrong.

"Just tired." That was true enough, and while he hated to keep things from his mom, this wasn't something he could discuss. Not until he knew more. People's reputations were on the line. As was his. Regardless of who had perpetuated the crime, it'd occurred on his watch.

"You just need a nice, home-cooked meal. How about Sunday night?"

"That sounds amazing." Some time with his parents, listening to his dad's crazy beekeeping stories, half of which he probably made up, would do his heart good.

"William Butterfield dropped half a cow off this morning, and Dad's talking about grilling some ribs. Enough for you and your brothers to take home leftovers."

"You don't have to do that. I *am* a grown man."

"A grown man who forgets to eat half the time and calls granola bars and sweet tea a well-rounded meal."

He laughed. "I'll have you know, I had a can of micro-waved chili a moment ago."

"Caden Alexander Stoughton, what am I ever going to do with you?"

"Just feed me."

"That's exactly what I'm fixing to do. Sunday night, six o'clock. And make sure to bring that pretty vet tech of yours and her sweet little one. Take them on that horse ride you promised but never delivered."

While his pulse accelerated at the thought, his brain told him to proceed with caution. "I'm sure she's got other plans." If Stephanie was the one stealing the drugs? He hated to think that way. Hated that he *had* to think that way.

"Doesn't hurt to ask."

"Guess not." If he argued, she'd think he was rude or she'd suspect something. It didn't seem right to speak sus-picions regarding a person when he had so little to go on. For all he knew, someone could've broken into the clinic and swapped the drugs then. Unlikely, sure, but possible.

He reached the clinic about ten minutes before Sher-iff Talbert, which gave Caden time to give the facility a once-over.

Paul was in the middle of mopping the lobby. He looked up when Caden entered.

"Hey, boss." He deposited his mop in the bucket, lifted his ball cap and raked a hand through his shaggy hair. "Wasn't expecting to see you in here tonight."

"I'm meeting someone."

"Oh?" Paul's T-shirt collar was stretched out and sweat stains shadowed his arms. While Caden would never ex-pect him to clean in his Sunday best, his appearance trig-gered more questions. He looked as haggard tonight as he had when he and Caden last spoke.

From grief or something else?

No. Paul was much too loyal to steal from them. Although…drugs could change a person. Make them do things they otherwise wouldn't.

Caden hated to think this way.

Talbert arrived just as Paul was heading out on his supper break, paper bag in hand. He was probably going to eat by the horse pastures, like he normally did.

Facing the sheriff, Caden relayed what he'd found along with his suspicions.

Talbert had numerous questions Caden didn't have answers for. Dr. Wallow and Lisa had handled their inventory. Why hadn't Lisa noticed the missing medication? Unless the theft had occurred since her last intake.

Or she was the culprit.

No. Not Lisa. She'd been at the clinic longer than he had and was one of their more loyal employees.

The sheriff looked over the receiving records. "Any chance the medications were swapped before they got to you?"

Caden shrugged. "We've dealt with the same deliveryman for going on three years, but I don't know the guy. Lisa managed that stuff."

"She work Monday?"

"Yeah. She'll be in by seven a.m."

"And your intern?"

His stomach sank. *Lord, please don't let this be her.* It couldn't be. "Yes. Same time."

Talbert gazed down the hall. "Paul Rider's been with you all for quite a while. What's he been like lately? Notice any changes in behavior?"

"More downcast and unkempt than normal, as I'd expect. We all lost a close friend, though Dr. Wallow's death probably hit Paul the hardest. Doc gave the fella a job when he was down on his luck. I don't know the full story, but I think he might've even paid for his car repairs, stuff like that, while the guy was getting his feet under him."

The officer frowned, as if considering Caden's words, then strode to the front door with focused intensity. "The lock here seems simple enough. You have an alarm an outsider would have to get past?"

Caden nodded. Dr. Wallow had often worked late—said he got more done when no one else was around to bug him. Could he have ever forgotten to set the alarm? "But whoever got into the medications would need to know the code to the safe also."

"You keep that information anywhere someone could find?"

"Wallow did." He explained, "But the notebook, all glittery and rainbow-colored, looked more like something one of his granddaughters would've left behind."

"You notice anyone poking around?"

"No one unexpected."

He relayed information regarding all the people who had been in and out of the office over the past six months or so.

"Any former employee we should be looking at?" the officer asked.

"Not really. I mean, we've had some volunteers come and go, but they were always supervised." Always? He wasn't certain he could say that. "And no one, other than Jeff, in the past year or so. We've had the same two people on staff—Lisa and Paul—since I've been here."

The officer widened his stance. "How often does Jeff come in?"

"Once or twice a week. He asked a few times about a possible job, but we never had the funds. Not to spend on an uneducated extra hand."

"How'd he take that?"

"Fine. He's been great." That kid was the last youth Caden would expect to do anything drug-related.

Talbert nodded and dropped his notebook back into his front pocket. "I'll need to talk to your staff Monday."

No doubt that would stir the rumor chain, challenging client trust even further. But what choice did he have? "Okay." At least he had the weekend to process everything and to pray.

"I'll need to drug test y'all, too."

Caden included? Though he'd known to expect as much, Talbert's statement reminded him that he'd likely be under as much suspicion as his staff, if not more.

"Bring your bank records and whatnot, as well."

"For the business or personal?"

"Both."

"No problem." He walked the sheriff to the door and shook his hand. "Thanks, Sheriff." Then he watched, jaw tense, as the man climbed into his vehicle and drove away.

It felt like the clinic was being hit by one problem after another. *Lord, I could really use Your help here.*

It'd take a miracle to keep this facility open.

Thankfully, he served a God who specialized in miracles. And as hard and discouraging as Caden's conversation with Talbert had been, one good thing had come from it. Stephanie wasn't the only suspect, or, it seemed, even the most likely.

Chapter Twelve

The early-evening sun filtered through the peach trees, dotting the grass with patches of light. The intermittent wind carried the scent of lilacs and an earthy aroma tinged with the smell of sunbaked peaches.

Maddy, her shiny braids bouncing against her back, chased after a butterfly. Laughter drifting from one of the "you-pick" groups captured her attention, and she stopped and stared. Stephanie followed her gaze to where nearly a quarter of the community, it seemed, milled about. The Herrons had hired a handful of youth to manage the scales and sales.

"You sure you don't need my help?" Stephanie waved a cluster of gnats away.

"Pshaw." Cassandra flicked a hand. "You focus on your internship and your little one. And taking time to heal."

After three years, it frustrated her to think she still had more healing to do, and yet she'd come a long way since she'd first decided to leave John. She'd been six months pregnant when he got arrested for killing a man in a bar fight. She'd realized that could've been her. Would've been her, and maybe Maddy, too, if she hadn't found a way to leave.

"Don't worry." She tucked a lock of hair behind her ear. "I've had extensive therapy."

"Oh, I know. While scrambling to survive. But here?" Cassandra motioned toward the distant hills. "Here you can rest, knowing you'll find food in the fridge, the electric bill will get paid, and the ground beneath you is sure."

"I'll be okay."

"I have no doubt. You're a strong woman who knows what she wants and has the gumption to get it. You know…" Cassandra rested her basket on her hip. "That little one could probably use some friends. Seems to me you could, too."

Stephanie had been thinking the same thing. She'd hoped to form connections at the women's group. The ladies had been super nice and welcoming, but it'd take more than one gathering for her to form relationships.

Truth was, she was lonely. About as lonely as when she was with her ex, only at least now she wasn't afraid. And while the Herrons had been amazing, Cassandra especially, Stephanie longed to connect with other moms her age. But she couldn't just show up at the coffeehouse, find a group of ladies and ask to join them.

"Mama blow it?" Maddy scampered over clutching a seeded dandelion.

Stephanie dropped to one knee and placed a hand on her daughter's shoulder. "Ready? Make a wish."

Maddy nodded and squeezed her eyes shut.

"One… Two…" On the count of three, Stephanie closed her hand over the tufts and quickly released them as if her daughter's soft breath, which lacked oomph, had scattered the seeds.

Maddy squealed and chased after the tufts floating on the breeze.

"The ladies from church have a painting night coming

up," Mrs. Herron said. "Gal named Faith—you remember her?"

"I'm not sure. I met a lot of people."

"She's a local artist. Hosts classes like those advertised in the city, only for free. Least this one is."

"I'm not very artistic."

"Then you'll fit right in."

Stephanie plucked a leaf from a low-lying branch. "Have you ever been to one of the Brewsters' fundraisers?"

Mrs. Herron's eyes glimmered. "Ah, that's right. The barn dance is tomorrow, isn't it?"

Face hot, her gaze faltered.

"You and Caden will have a wonderful time." The sparkle in her eyes suggested she thought, or maybe hoped, the event would turn romantic.

The idea sent a stampede of butterflies traipsing through Stephanie's midsection. She gave what she hoped to be a casual shrug. "We're going to network is all."

Cassandra nodded and donned a serious expression, though her hint of a smile indicated she wasn't convinced. "A gal can never have too many friends or connections. Maybe you'll run into a local rancher looking to hire."

"Maybe."

Her shelter friends had encouraged her to choose a more "sensible" career like office admin, and not merely because they'd been surrounded by concrete, buildings and freeways. Vet tech hours were long and unpredictable, which could make single parenting exponentially more challenging.

Stephanie had spent nearly a lifetime giving up on herself. Not anymore. She wanted to experience how it felt to truly live.

"This will be good for you." Cassandra wrapped an arm around her shoulder. "You and Caden will have a great time."

Her pulse quickened as his kind, lopsided smile and hazel eyes came to mind. Her and Caden. Together, at a dance.

Where they'd likely dance. Together.

She wanted to pretend this was just a dance. And maybe for him it was. But for her, it felt like so much more. Freedom. New beginnings. And a night with one of the kindest men she'd met in some time.

"Well, lookee there." Cassandra pointed.

Stephanie turned to see Vincent approaching in his big floppy straw hat.

"Ladies." He kissed his wife's cheek, then gave Maddy a high five. "Thought I saw you three moseying around. Eatin' the crop, I see." Smiling, he picked Maddy up, swung her over his shoulder, then dropped her, giggling, back onto her feet.

He turned to Stephanie. "One of our seasonal workers was talking about a rancher looking for help. Not a vet per se, but someone knowledgeable regarding vaccines, basic wound care and whatnot."

He pulled a slip of paper from his pocket and handed it over. "Tell this fella Vincent sent you his way."

Stephanie smiled. "Thanks." It encouraged her to know the Herrons were pulling for her.

"You best get, young lady." Cassandra made a shooing motion. "I'll watch your nugget."

"You sure?"

"Yep."

"Shouldn't I wait until Monday?"

"Nah. Evening's probably the best time to call a rancher. Matter of fact, bet he's just about to sit down for supper. Now scoot."

Laughing, Stephanie did as told, anxious to follow up on the first real lead she'd received. With how much Sage Creek folks admired the Herrons, having Vincent's name behind her would mean a lot. Maybe even enough to warrant a job offer.

Her hopes were dashed, however, before she had a chance to relay her credentials.

Phone to her ear, Stephanie tried to keep her voice cheerful. "I understand your concern." The rancher's assumptions, however, were false. "But nowadays, more than sixty percent of vets are women."

"I thought you said you're a tech."

"I am. I just meant—"

"Those women veterinarians work with bulls? Because that's a whole lot of muscle to deal with."

"Some, yes."

"Where'd you say you got my number?"

"From Mr. Herron."

"Guess I need to be more specific regarding qualifications."

"Sir?"

"Thank you for calling."

In other words, buzz off. The man had decided against her the moment he heard her voice. Was that how the other ranchers would respond? Did they assume ranch hands had to be male?

Taking advantage of her unexpected free time, Stephanie sat in the grass, pulled up the internet on her phone and navigated to a job site.

While she found a handful of openings, none were all that close to her mom. That would mean uprooting Maddy, again, only without a solid place to land. Unless she found something spectacular, it seemed her best option was to remain with the Herrons.

Assuming they let her and Maddy stay. But what if another woman and child were waiting?

An incoming call startled her, and she checked the screen. Rhonda Chandler? As she remembered the break-in, her chest tightened. She stared at the phone, unmoving. What if her location had been compromised or something had happened to one of the other ladies?

She wiped a clammy hand on her thigh and answered. "Hello?"

"Good evening. I hope I'm not calling at a bad time?"

"Not at all." *Breathe. In. Out.*

"The police confirmed our suspicions. The perpetrator was an angry former resident. While she caused significant damage, they feel certain we have no cause for concern regarding our confidential files."

Stephanie exhaled, her relief so intense, it triggered tears. "That's great news. Thank you for calling."

"Of course. You have a great—"

"Mrs. Chandler?"

"Yes?"

"My stay with the Herrons. Is there any way I can extend it?"

She paused. "We try to honor our original agreements with our host families. How much longer were you hoping to stay?"

"I'm not sure." She explained her situation.

"We can help you find employment opportunities. I'll send you a form tomorrow."

That should encourage her, but all she could think about was the fact that she'd no longer see Caden.

Caden aside, the clinic seemed her best prospect. She'd basically been "interviewing" daily. Plus, he appeared pleased with her. His only concern seemed to be related to all the changes that had occurred or might occur due to Dr. Wallow's death.

She could certainly empathize with his situation.

"I appreciate that," Stephanie said. "I just think, if I wait a little longer, maybe Cad—Dr. Stoughton will have found his new normal and will feel more comfortable adding to his staff."

"Is something else going on, Stephanie?"

"Like what?"

"It's common for women to struggle to stand on their own, after being controlled for so long. They land right back into another bad situation."

"Oh, no. I've come much too far for that."

She paused again. "Let me talk with the team and the Herrons."

"Thank you."

Stephanie pocketed her phone and returned to the house. The sound of Southern gospel drifting from the kitchen indicated Cassandra and Maddy were back. Cassandra's soft vibrato singing along carried a deep sense of joy and peace.

A joy and peace that felt contagious and characterized the woman and her home. Traits Stephanie hoped to take with her, once she and Maddy had their own place.

In the kitchen, Cassandra sat at the table with Maddy on her lap, memory-matching cards spread before them.

Cassandra smiled at Stephanie as she entered, then flipped one of the cards over. "What's that?"

"Fishy!" Maddy's torso sprang forward.

"Close. That's a dolphin, and they live in the sea."

"Dolphin?"

"Yep." She scanned the remaining overturned cards. "Now, where do you think his match is? Right here?" She pointed at a card, and Maddy vigorously shook her head.

"This one?"

Another head shake.

Stephanie joined them at the table.

"How about here?" Cassandra pointed again.

"Yeah! Yeah! Yeah!" Maddy bounced in her lap.

Cassandra flipped the card over, revealing a purple-and-green cat. "Ah. Bummer. Your turn."

Stephanie joined in until Maddy decided she was done, wiggled down and ambled off toward her toy box in the living room.

Cassandra stood. "Well, guess I best get started on supper." She began pulling ingredients from the cupboard and fridge. "Mind washing the lettuce?"

"Gladly." Stephanie went to the sink to clean her hands, thinking back to similar nights she'd spent in her mother's kitchen. As much as she enjoyed Cassandra, she missed her mom terribly. She would've been out for a visit already, if only she could get the time off or either of them could spare the travel expense.

Maybe come Christmas, once Stephanie had found a job and saved up some money.

Cassandra planted her hands on her hips. "Think Rheanna would like to serve some of my cobblers at that barn dance of hers?"

"I'm sure she'd be thrilled and so very grateful." Stephanie added lettuce leaves to the spinner.

"We Sage Creek folks like to band together." She peeled a garlic clove. "Like Pastor always says, there's power in numbers." She wiped her hands on her apron and surveyed her un-chopped vegetables. "Sure wish I'd purchased more tomatoes. Might have to modify my sauce recipe."

"I can run to the store."

"I hate to ask you to do that. I know your at-home time is worth guarding."

"It's no bother." Her daughter now sat on the floor, playing with an old cloth doll. "Maddy's occupied, and the drive into town will give me time to think."

She'd been considering the pastor's sermon in light of all she'd experienced since leaving her ex-husband. Maybe God hadn't abandoned her after all.

In fact, He'd sent a lot of people to help her, the Herrons included.

And Caden?

Cassandra pulled a notepad and pen from her junk drawer. "Would you mind picking up a few other things while you're there?"

"Not at all."

"You're such a blessing." She handed Stephanie a list of items along with some cash. "Tomatoes are on sale two for a dollar. I can't remember the last time I bought them for that price. Figure we might as well stock up. And take my car so you're not using your own gas."

"You sure?"

"'Course. Wouldn't want it to cost you to run me an errand now, would I?"

Considering all the Herrons had done for her, gas spent running to town and back seemed like more than a fair trade. But Stephanie knew the woman well enough to know there was no sense arguing with her.

And so, Stephanie humbly thanked her.

Outside, a thin layer of overcast dimmed the sky to a faded teal-gray dotted with patches of thicker clouds. The wind had picked up considerably, causing the peach tree branches to dip and sway in the distance.

By the time she reached the store, the temperature had dropped at least ten degrees. It'd be a perfect night to sit out on the porch with sweet little Maddy.

Stepping out of her car, she watched two ladies and two children walk across the lot, each child holding one of the women's hands. The older of the two appeared to be in her fifties, and the younger close to Stephanie's age. The four of them together made her miss her mom all the more.

Her phone rang. She glanced at the return number and answered. "Hey, I was just thinking of you."

"Good thoughts, I hope." Her mom's voice carried a smile.

"Always." What she wouldn't give to be talking to her

in person right now, over a steaming mug of coffee. "I've got a long list of rom-coms we need to watch together."

"I'm saving up to head your way, baby girl."

"Assuming I stay in Sage Creek."

"Still no word on the vet tech job?"

"Not really." She relayed her last conversation with Caden.

Her mom didn't answer right away, and when she did, her tone seemed guarded. "That could be promising."

"You sound concerned."

"Just worry about you, being so far away and all."

"I'm sorry."

"For what? Me being a fretting mama?"

"For my past giving you reason to worry." She could only imagine how hard it had been for her mom, knowing how much her daughter had struggled and watching her fight her way back. She wasn't sure how she'd react if Maddy had gone through the same ordeal.

"Sweet girl, you have no reason to apologize. I'm proud of you and where you are. All you've overcome." She paused. "A friend forwarded me an email of a job opening in Cleveland. An adoption coordinator position at an animal shelter. I know it's not really what you're looking for, but it could lead to something better."

Maybe she did need to start looking for entry-level positions, except that she'd need more than an entry-level income. "What's the pay?"

"Probably not nearly enough. Any chance those people from that Next Steps program can help you find housing again?"

"I don't think so. There are probably other ladies waiting for help. And I doubt they have anything in Cleveland. Plus, I'd rather not bounce Maddy from home to home, if I can help it."

"You know you both can always stay with me."

"Where would we sleep?" Her mom lived in a tiny studio barely big enough to store her belongings.

"You two could take the bedroom. I'd sleep on the couch."

"I can't do that to you."

"It'd be no bother, really. Besides, it'd only be temporary. Until you found steady employment."

Maybe her mom was right. But she'd held such hopes for this internship. She'd even allowed herself to grow attached to the Texas Hill Country, with all its wildflowers and lush green pastures. This was definitely the type of environment she'd love to raise Maddy in.

If she left, she'd never see Caden again. The thought weighed heavy on her. Too heavy.

"Just think about it," her mom said. "Am I video-calling in tonight to read sweet Maddy girl a bedtime story?"

"She'd love that." She ended the call and followed a teenage couple into the store.

A gust of cold air poured down upon her as she entered, and eighties rock music played from hidden speakers. She scanned the list Cassandra had given her, then her surroundings. Produce to her right, crackers and other snacks nearly dead center. She'd head that way in a moment, but first, she veered left to check out the store's community board.

Nothing worth noting among the few jobs posted. Someone was looking for a house cleaner. Someone else wanted a biweekly dog walker. A poster advertising the horse rescue's fundraising event occupied a large section in the center, triggering thoughts of her and Caden together on the dance floor. His firm hand on her back, the musky scent of his aftershave invading her senses. His breath, which always seemed to smell like mints, warm on her cheek.

Laughter behind her jolted her back to the present. Clearing her throat, she snatched a tear-off tab from a flyer for a live-in nanny—just in case, and assuming they didn't have a problem with Maddy.

Then again, if it came to that, they might as well stay with her mom. Stephanie would be temporarily out of an income but the rent-free living and support would give her time to job search.

She'd love to stay on at the clinic, but Caden seemed to be struggling. He'd obviously lost much more than another vet when Dr. Wallow had died. Granted, even the most competent businessman would experience a transitional period after something like that. But what if he didn't have the ability to run a practice?

What if he hired her, she and Maddy got settled, and he lost the clinic?

With a sigh, she grabbed her cart and strode to the cereal aisle. Ten minutes later, she stood in front of a large bin of shiny red tomatoes sold for more than double what Cassandra had told her.

Her hands felt clammy, her lungs tightening as images from an evening six months into her marriage flashed through her mind. She'd gone to the store earlier that day and selected fresh herbs to prepare John's favorite meal— chicken Parmesan. She'd arrived home, arms loaded with groceries, to find her husband standing in the kitchen, beer in hand. Crushed beer cans she hadn't remembered being there before filled the nearby garbage can.

She struggled for air, her breath coming in short bursts. Gripping her cart, she fought against a wave of dizziness the flashback brought.

John had looked angrier than she'd ever seen him. He'd demanded to know where she'd been and accused her of spending all "his" money. He said it was her fault their checks had bounced. She'd tried to tell him she'd merely gone shopping, but that had fueled his rage. That was when he'd beaten her for the first time. That was the night she should've left.

"Stephanie, hi."

It took a moment for Caden's voice to register. She took a deep breath to regain composure, then faced him with a forced smile. "Caden. Good to see you." She glanced into his cart, empty except for a large box of fruit-twists cereal, chocolate milk, potato chips and bananas. "Hungry?" She'd intended a teasing tone, but lingering unpleasant memories made her voice wobble.

He offered his adorably sheepish smile. "Now you see why my mom's always trying to feed me." He adjusted his cowboy hat. "Speaking of, she asked if I'd relay an invite to dinner, with horseback riding after. Figure I should make good on my promise to that princess of yours sooner rather than later."

Another evening with Caden at his parents' beautiful and peaceful homestead? Her heart leaped at the thought. But she retained her composure. "That sounds lovely. When was she thinking?"

"Sometime after the barn dance most likely." A slight blush colored his otherwise chiseled cheeks.

Was he looking forward to their time together as much as she was? And if so, what then? She sensed he wasn't the kind of guy to date casually, nor was she looking for that. But had he fully considered what he'd be taking on should they become romantically involved? Was he prepared to be a father?

She was getting ahead of herself. They hadn't even gone on an official date, and honestly, she wasn't even sure how Caden felt about her. Yes, she often caught him watching her throughout the day, although lately, there'd been times when his expression displayed suspicion.

She understood that. He was considering her for employment.

At least, she believed he was. Felt nearly certain of that. But that would add a whole new level of complications were they to date, him being her boss and all.

His phone rang. He glanced at the screen and frowned. Visibly tensing, he excused himself, moving toward the lettuce bins, to answer. Though she'd only heard the first snippet of the conversation, she thought he'd referred to the caller as Sheriff. That and his sudden change of body language suggested something was wrong. She hoped nothing major, and not just for job-security reasons. The poor guy had been hit with enough already. She'd need to find ways to be more helpful. And to add joy and laughter, the best stress relievers ever, into his days.

If he stole her heart in the process?

She was beginning to fear he already had.

Chapter Thirteen

❧

Stephanie swept Maddy's nose, cheeks and forehead with the soft bristles of her makeup brush. "There. Now you're all prettied up."

Maddy stood taller, eyes gleaming. "That, too, pwease?" She pointed to Stephanie's coral-tinted lip gloss.

"Absolutely! Every princess needs glittery lips."

Maddy's grin bunched her cheeks. Then she puckered her mouth in an exaggerated pout that made it hard for Stephanie to keep from laughing.

She dabbed some gloss on Maddy's lips, then angled her head, hands on her hips. "Pure perfection."

"Pewfesion?" Eyebrows pulled together, Maddy tilted her head.

"You're adorable, you know that?"

With seriousness, Maddy nodded.

Stephanie laughed and checked the time on her phone. "You ready for your ice cream date with MeeMaw and PawPaw?"

"Yes!" Hands fisted at her sides, Maddy bounced on the balls of her feet and bolted from the room, calling out to Cassandra, "MeeMaw, come see me!"

"Come show us, sweet pea," Vincent's deep yet gentle voice called back.

It touched Stephanie deeply that the Herrons allowed Maddy to call them MeeMaw and PawPaw. She'd overheard one of the kids visiting the "you-pick" section call her grandparents that and had immediately declared that she wanted a MeeMaw and PawPaw, too. Stephanie had tried to explain that she already had a grandmother, but she shook her head and said, "No. A MeeMaw and PawPaw."

Stephanie thought for sure the girl was going to throw a tantrum. She probably would have if Cassandra hadn't interjected, saying she'd gladly be Maddy's MeeMaw. The wide grin Maddy gave her in response both lifted Stephanie's heart and stung, revealing yet another hole in her daughter's life. Stephanie appreciated all the ways Cassandra and her husband loved Maddy. But she also knew, the closer they and her daughter became, the harder it'd be on her should they have to move.

Hopefully, it wouldn't come to that.

She glanced in the mirror one more time, almost taken aback by her reflection. The bright-eyed, smiling woman who stared back at her was such a stark contrast to the almost lifeless image displayed in her car's rearview mirror the night she'd left John. She'd felt so numb, depleted and defeated. How she wanted to believe good awaited her and the precious baby growing inside her, but she'd been too afraid to hope.

And here she stood, almost giddy with anticipation for her date—which most certainly wasn't a date.

She needed to stop acting like such a silly schoolgirl. Caden was her boss. Her boss who could soon cut her loose, if she wasn't careful. Tonight, she had to demonstrate the people skills and professionalism that would make him want to keep her. Allowing her thoughts to become entangled in romantic fantasies wouldn't help her efforts.

With a deep breath, she followed her joyful daughter into the living room. Cassandra was folding a hamper of laundry, and Vincent was flipping through one of his outdoorsman magazines.

"Wow." Setting a towel on her pile, Cassandra looked from Stephanie to Maddy, then back to Stephanie. "Two beautiful girls." Hands on her knees, she leaned toward Maddy. "Is that lip gloss you're wearing?"

Maddy nodded and pushed her lips out.

"Very pretty." She faced Stephanie, affection radiating from her eyes. "You ready for tonight?"

Stephanie breathed deep and nodded.

"I'm proud of you for going."

"It's no big deal."

"Oh, it is. It's a huge step, one that's probably got your stomach tied in knots, for numerous reasons. And I'm proud of you."

"Me, too." Vincent gave her shoulder a playful punch.

She was so appreciative for the support these two continually gave her. To know they understood meant so much. "Thank you."

Cassandra squeezed her hand, then grabbed her purse from the coffee table. "Guess we're all set."

Stephanie resisted the urge to chew her bottom lip, which would only smear her gloss. She was half tempted to ditch the barn dance and join her daughter and the Herrons for their ice cream outing. She wasn't sure what made her more nervous—attending her first real social event since John or spending the evening with Caden.

Cassandra paused, worry lines deepening on her forehead. "Would you like us to wait with you, until Caden gets here?"

"I'll be fine. Besides, I'm not sure Maddy could contain herself much longer."

She was once again bouncing on the balls of her feet, looking about ready to burst.

"I almost forgot." Cassandra snapped her fingers. "We'd

like to offer Caden free booth space at the peach festival. To promote the clinic."

"That's very kind of you."

"It's the neighborly thing to do. Besides, with all the summers he worked out here as a young man, we owe him as much. Mention it tonight. Tell him to call us if he has questions."

"Okay." Stephanie dropped to Maddy's eye level and smoothed her bangs from her face. "You be good now." She kissed her forehead.

Cassandra took Maddy's hand and gave a cheery wave, and the two followed Vincent out and into his truck.

Stephanie watched them leave, her hands growing clammy.

What would tonight be like? How many people would be there? Would Caden ask her to dance? Seemed logical, it being a dance and all. An image of the two of them together, her hand in his, his other hand on the small of her back, came to mind, sending a rush of warmth through her.

But what if someone else asked her to dance, as well? What if she froze up or, worse, had a panic attack? She'd be mortified.

Chest tight, she paced the Herrons' small living room as numerous scenarios ran through her mind.

Stop it.

This was not helping. She was a grown woman, for goodness' sake. She'd faced a lot more frightening things than a rural fundraising dance. If she could escape her ex, earn a degree as a single mom, and move her and her daughter halfway across the country, she could certainly two-step with Caden and whoever else happened to be there.

She'd barely sat when she heard the sound of gravel crunched beneath tires. She closed her eyes briefly, grabbed her purse and opened the door.

Caden stepped out of his truck in his signature charcoal cowboy hat, boots, jeans and a short-sleeve denim shirt.

"Evening." He tipped his hat with a hint of a smile, then hurried to open the passenger-side door.

As she approached, his musky cologne ignited her senses and accelerated her pulse. She looked up into his hazel-green eyes. The gold flecks in his irises seemed more pronounced.

For a moment, he seemed to freeze, completely focused on her.

"You look nice." His voice sounded husky. He cleared his throat, and with a half step back, shut her door.

She set her purse on the floorboard and fastened her seat belt. Hands on her knees, she waited while he rounded the truck and climbed in beside her. Reminding herself that tonight was merely business did nothing to quiet her jitters.

"You ready for some hee-hawing?" He shot her a grin and threw the truck in Reverse.

She laughed. "Sure. I guess."

"There might even be square dancing." He turned onto the long gravel road flanked by cypress trees interspersed with dandelions, clover and purple horsemint blooms. "You ever been?"

"Square dancing?"

He nodded.

She shook her head, envisioning older women dressed in multicolored flouncy skirts and men in matching button-down shirts she'd seen at county fairs.

"Don't worry. You'll catch on soon enough." He turned onto the two-lane highway that led to the horse rescue.

"Do people often host barn dances around here?"

"Some, yeah. To celebrate anniversaries, sweet sixteen birthdays, that sort of thing."

"Is that how you celebrated your birthday?"

"Hardly. A buddy and I went camping, two teenagers

trying to act like a couple of rough and tough mountain men." He chuckled. "Mom wanted to send us off with sandwiches, potato chips and granola bars. But we wanted to fish for our food. We did, however, accept slices of birthday cake wrapped in tinfoil. Good thing, too, because that cake was our only meal."

"Didn't catch anything?"

"Nothing but weeds. 'Course, we blamed that on the river."

"Of course. Where'd you go?"

"We drove twenty minutes east till we reached a place we liked along the river. We were trespassing on someone's property, but we didn't think about that. Just headed out with our gear, a machete and high expectations."

She raised her eyebrows. "A machete?"

"To forge our trail through the uncharted wilderness." Mirth lighted his voice.

She laughed. "Ah. Of course."

He cast her a sideways glance. "What about you? How'd you spend your sweet sixteen?"

That seemed like such a long time ago, back when she'd had such lofty dreams for her life, such anticipation for her future. No real sense of fear to speak of. So much had changed. She had changed, and not always in good ways. But step by step, she was regaining herself, and maybe even regaining her sense of wonder. Of hope-filled anticipation.

"My mom threw me a party, with a 'night in Paris' theme. She went all out. Spent way more than she could afford as a single mom, I'm sure. Even took me shopping for a new dress. That was my favorite part—shopping together, laughing over lunch after while she shared stories from her teen years."

The sign for the horse rescue, decorated with white, gold and purple balloons, came into view. They followed a car coming from the other way onto a winding dirt road that led to the stables and barn. Other vehicles, at least three dozen, were parked in the drive and on the grassy areas on either side.

"You and your mom sound close," he said.

Tears pricked her eyes. "We are." When she first left her husband, her mom's daily phone calls—pep talks and words of encouragement—had helped hold her together. Made her believe she could make something of herself.

"You miss her?"

She nodded. Even more than she thought she would. "She always knows the right thing to say. Makes me feel like I can do about anything. Be just about anything."

He parked, then shifted to face her. "You can." His gaze dropped to her mouth, and she held her breath. But then he turned off the engine and opened his door. "Guess it's showtime, huh?"

Right. He'd invited her here for work purposes.

Not to fall in love with the kind, handsome and gentle man who had managed to completely capture her heart.

When they entered the decorated barn, Caden could practically feel Stephanie's excitement. Her eyes sparkled as she surveyed the buffet table lining the east wall. It was made from wine barrels covered with a large plank of wood. On eating tables occupying the other half of the room, candles flickered in lace-and-burlap-adorned mason jars. Twinkle lights draped from the rafters, bathing the interior in a soft glow.

"You hungry?" he asked.

"I might be too nervous."

"Don't worry. These people will love you." As the saying went, to know her was to love her. With each day he spent with her, those words became increasingly true.

But what about the missing drugs? He couldn't believe

she was to blame, but neither could he exclude the possibility.

All he knew was he didn't want it to be her. Because, as much as he fought against it, he couldn't deny he had feelings for her.

"How about we get us some of those fancy appetizers over there." He pointed to a barrel covered with a lacy white tablecloth. "Then I'll introduce you to folks."

She offered that shy smile he'd grown to love. "Sounds like a plan."

He looked around at the many familiar faces, most from Sage Creek and at least a handful of former clients. He needed to chat with them, find out why they'd stopped coming in.

As to those he didn't recognize, he figured there was a fifty-fifty chance they had animals. No, make that seventy-thirty. This was a horse rescue fundraising event, after all.

"Mrs. Herron wanted me to tell you that they're reserving booth space for you at the festival, free of charge." Stephanie accompanied him to three towers of onion rings, each maybe fifteen rings tall. "So you can promote the clinic."

"Yeah? That's awesome." People came to the event from all around, maybe too far to be familiar with him or the clinic but close enough to pop in, if they had a need.

She nodded and spooned blue cheese sauce onto her plate.

"You want to help man the booth? We always close the clinic during the peach festival." Nearly the entire town shut down for local events. Sometimes that felt frustrating, but mostly he valued how much everyone prioritized community. He appreciated that, even when traditions hit his pocketbook.

"I'll have to figure out what to do with Maddy, but sure. I'd love to."

Most likely, someone from Faith Trinity's quilting club would snatch that child for the day. They'd fill her with laughter and cotton candy, then drop her off content and droopy-eyed. That was another thing he loved about Sage Creek folks—how they supported one another, those with kids especially.

They spent the next hour or so talking with people, and Caden made two new promising connections and engaged in a productive conversation with a client who had left their clinic a year prior.

The DJ urged everyone to get their "honky-tonk" on, as he called it. At first, only a few couples responded. But by the third song, most everyone had migrated to the dance floor.

Stephanie seemed highly entertained by the growing crowd doing the Electric Slide. He loved watching the way she laughed whenever someone stumbled over their steps or acted silly. How she leaned forward, as if enthralled, when everyone's steps picked up. Her expression of almost childlike delight when an older couple wearing matching outfits took center stage.

There was no way she could be hooked on drugs, or trying to sell them for that matter. She was too sweet. Too innocent.

Wasn't she?

Then the music slowed, and about half the dancers returned to their seat.

Stephanie turned back to the table and took a sip of her sweet tea. Set her glass down, then took another drink.

He should ask her to dance. It'd seem normal, wouldn't it? Maybe even expected? But what if she said no, or worse, said yes because she felt obligated to. He swallowed, his hands suddenly clammy. He'd look the fool.

But he'd be an even bigger fool if he let this night, this moment, slip by.

He gave a nervous cough and dropped his napkin on the table. "Figure I can't let you leave tonight without giving you the full barn dance experience." The words came out before his brain had a chance to stop them. "What do you say?" He stood and held out his hand, half wishing he'd kept his big mouth shut.

A soft smile lit her face. "I'd like that."

He felt a sudden urge to make a fist pump. Instead, he calmly took her delicate hand in his and led her out to the dance floor.

At first, she seemed stiff, uncertain and reluctant to make eye contact. So he started talking—about the band, a group of guys who'd graduated from high school a couple years ahead of him. About one of the ranchers, a friend of the family who'd had him, his dad and his brothers over for skeet shooting numerous times when he was growing up. And about the early days of the horse rescue.

"To think, if not for that flood, and that emergency rescue, those two might never have reunited," she said. "The entire story is so romantic. Like it came straight out of a novel or something."

"Guess when it's meant to be, it's meant to be, huh?"

She studied him for a moment, her expression unreadable, and he wondered if she was thinking the same thing he was, feeling what he was. More than that, he wondered when he'd get up the nerve to ask. But in not knowing, there was hope.

If he voiced his emotions and she didn't feel the same, what then?

A male voice, angry, rose to their left, and the talking surrounding them ceased. He turned to see Maxwell, a guy one of his brothers used to hang around with, yelling at some other guy. Caden only caught bits of the conversation, but it sounded like Maxwell felt cheated out of something and was ready to throw blows.

"That man can be such a jerk." He shook his head. "One would think—"

Her face looked tight, her eyes wide.

"You okay?" He touched her elbow. She flinched and hugged her torso. "Stephanie, what's wrong?"

"I need some fresh air." She darted off, zigzagging through the crowd, and disappeared out the barn doors.

He stared after her. What had just happened?

"Caden, my man."

A hand fell on his shoulder.

"Excuse me." He pushed his way through people and out into the inky night, searching for Stephanie.

A shadowed form sat against the trunk of a tree about fifty yards away. Gravel and twigs crunched beneath his boots as he made his way to her. Silver moonlight caressed her face and shimmered on her sleek hair.

"Mind if I join you?" he asked.

She motioned to the ground beside her, and he sat, the two of them in silence for a moment.

"I'm sorry about that." Her voice seemed to catch, as if she was fighting tears. "You must think I'm strange. Unstable."

"Upset about something, but not unstable." He paused. "Want to talk about it?"

She didn't respond.

"Did I do something?" He mentally replayed the moments leading to her rapid exit.

"It's not you. It's..." She plucked a blade of grass from the ground. "No. You've been perfect." She gave a weak, almost sad smile. After a long pause, she said, "That man's anger. It... I'm a domestic abuse survivor."

"What do you mean?"

"My ex-husband. He used to...take his anger out on me. Using his fists." And then, it all came out. The things John had said, how they'd cut so deeply, and the all-consuming fear that had overshadowed her for so long. "I guess I'm still learning to catch my breath."

He felt like he'd been punched in the gut. "I'm so sorry." Was that why she seemed so nervous all the time? Why, when they'd first met, she'd stiffened whenever she climbed into the truck with him or stood near him? "Where is he now?" A surge of anger shot through him, followed by a fierce desire to come to her defense.

"California. He doesn't know where I am."

He took in a deep breath and released it slowly, forcing his tense muscles to relax. As much as he wanted to pummel the guy for hurting such a delicate creature as Stephanie, she needed him now.

He placed his arm around her shoulder. She stiffened. Then, with an exhale, she leaned into him.

If only they could remain like this, him holding her and her tucked so securely in his embrace.

One thing he knew for certain—no man would hurt her ever again if he had anything to say about it.

Chapter Fourteen

For the second night in a row, Stephanie found herself standing in front of the mirror, preparing for an evening with Caden. Granted, he hadn't initiated either event. Rheanna had invited her to the barn dance, and his mom had asked her to dinner.

So why had she spent the past thirty minutes fighting with her hair? Today's increased humidity wasn't helping, to say the least. If she had more time, she'd jump back in the shower and start over.

She wasn't sure what made her stomach more jittery—the fact that she'd be spending additional time with Caden or his parents. Regardless of how kind and welcoming the Stoughtons had been last time, they were still Caden's parents. She wanted them to like her, now more than ever.

Because she was beginning to think that maybe, just maybe, she and Caden could actually have something between them. That they were, in fact, building something.

She closed her eyes, remembering how he'd led her around the makeshift dance floor. The feel of his strong, steady arm on her back, the scent of his cologne and the rhythmic beating of his heart when she'd lost herself in his arms and had rested her head against his chest. The way he'd peered down at her, as if she were the most beautiful woman in the room.

That was precisely how he'd made her feel.

She'd felt so safe, so completely captivated, she'd momentarily forgotten where they were and why they went to the dance.

Yet the memory that stuck with her most was when he'd come outside to find her. She'd been mortified and had wanted nothing more than for him to leave her alone. Instead, he sat beside her, not pushing her to explain herself or shaming her for her reaction. Just sitting quietly, acting like there was nowhere else he'd rather be.

She couldn't remember when she'd felt that way around a man.

A soft rap on wood startled her, and she looked up to see Cassandra standing in her open doorway.

"Beautiful as ever." She smiled. "If the sight of you doesn't plumb knock Caden off his feet, I don't know what will. Though I imagine you did that last night already." Mischief twinkled in her eyes.

"He's my boss, Ms. Cassandra."

"Want to talk it out?"

Off-key singing flowed in from the other room, Maddy's high-pitched lisp merging with Vincent's baritone. That man had been such a blessing, in so many ways. Had Stephanie had such a positive male role model in her life growing up, maybe she wouldn't have gotten messed up with her ex. Her mom had done her best but hadn't had much time or interest for a romantic relationship.

Stephanie spritzed her hair with hair spray, then set the canister down. "Talk what out?"

"You and Caden. Whatever's going on there and whatever your relationship with him is stirring up."

"I'm okay. And I wouldn't really call this a relationship."

"Sure seems to be heading that way."

Her face heated.

"How do you feel about that?"

"I guess I'm just sort of taking things as they come." She picked up her makeup brush. "You've known Caden for a while?"

"Since he was a wee one, though we got to know him best in his teen years, once he started working here."

"Why isn't he married?"

"Guess no woman's managed to snatch him up." She chuckled. "Though he was engaged once. He fell hard into love and even harder into heartache when she up and bailed on him. Don't know the whole story, but I heard she hurt him pretty bad."

"How long ago was that?"

"Five years or so. But he never seemed interested in dating after that. I suspect he hasn't had time, what with tending to his patients and all. That is, until now." She offered a teasing smile.

She crossed the room to where Stephanie stood and held her by her shoulders. "Any man, Caden included, would be lucky to have you and that precious little one of yours. Remember that."

"John always told me how worthless I was. And I knew in my head that wasn't true, but after a while…"

"You started to believe it."

She gave a slight shrug.

"And now?"

"I'm becoming reacquainted with who I was before I met John."

"God's brought you a long way, sweet girl."

Stephanie thought about something Kayla Williams had said during the women's group meeting a week ago. *Everyone has stuff. But so long as you keep moving forward, keep turning to Jesus…*

Stephanie needed to learn how to turn to Him. She bit her bottom lip. "Would you mind praying with me?"

"Absolutely." Cassandra took Stephanie's hand in her own. "About what, sweetie?"

"I don't know. That I do the right thing. For Maddy and me. And that God helps me find steady employment." And that she had the courage, if Caden truly was the one, to give him her heart completely.

And if he wasn't?

"I can do that." Cassandra bowed her head.

Stephanie did the same, and for the first time in as long as she could remember, she honestly prayed. As she did, a sense of peace washed over her, along with a deep understanding that she was going to be okay. That God was with her, was leading her and wouldn't abandon her.

Like Mrs. Williams had said, so long as she kept running to Jesus, rather than from Him, she'd be okay. Regardless of how things turned out between her and Caden, she needn't ever be alone.

In his father's workshop, Caden swept sawdust into a dustpan while his oldest brother gathered spare nails and screws and deposited them in their respective receptacles. Their bee farm was doing so well, his parents decided to increase their storage capacity.

Dad stepped back and surveyed the shelves they'd just made. "It'll do. Thanks, boys." He started stacking the containers of honey according to type and loaded those labeled "Chunk Honey" into a wooden crate. "Would you boys mind carrying these to the store? Mom's got orders to ship out tomorrow."

Caden checked the time on his phone. Stephanie and her adorable daughter would arrive soon. "I've got a few minutes."

Dad smiled. "That's right. I forgot you're having a girl

over for dinner." With a chuckle, he clamped a hand on Caden's shoulder.

Caden's face heated. "It's not like that." But he wanted it to be, and he was beginning to think, or at least hope, that perhaps she did, too. Maybe tonight he'd have the courage to ask her. "Mom invited her, remember?"

"Semantics." Dad winked.

Shaking his head, Caden hefted a filled crate out of the storage shed and into the hot sun. The air felt heavy, sticky with humidity, and smelled of baked earth and fresh-cut grass. Wispy clouds drifted across the pale blue sky.

His brother Terry fell into step beside him. "How serious are things between you two?"

"Me and Stephanie?"

Terry nodded.

Caden wasn't sure how he wanted to answer that. "She's a nice girl. Smart." Compassionate and beautiful. A wonderful mother.

He sensed Terry studying him.

Caden stopped and faced his brother. "What?"

"Mom told me about the theft at your clinic."

"Why do I sense an unasked question in that statement?"

"What's her story?"

"Not my business."

"Seems to me it should be, you being her boss and all."

His grip on his crate tightened. "What are you getting at?"

"Just be careful. And alert."

"It wasn't her."

"You sure about that? Because the timing seems fishy, if you ask me."

"You know nothing about her." Then again, neither did he. Not really. But he knew enough. The sweetness in her eyes. The tender way she cared for her daughter. How gentle she was with patients. Regardless of what brought her here, what her life had been like prior, she'd demonstrated nothing but character since she'd been here.

She wasn't the type to steal narcotics.

He thought back to her reaction at the dance. And then about the night he ran into her at the grocery store. She'd stood, frozen, in front of those tomatoes. He'd watched her for a few moments, and she'd seemed so tense. Checking the items in her cart, looking at the tomatoes, then back to her cart. Her actions had seemed strange.

He'd wondered about her fear. Now he knew.

How could anyone hurt a vulnerable woman? She'd obviously overcome a lot. Had maybe even left the guy with little to nothing to her name. And here she was, working on an intern's salary. That had to be tough.

They reached the family store, which was little more than a one-room shed decorated with interior lights and flower arrangements inside and out. He marched around to the storage area his father had built and deposited his crate.

Turning back around, he nearly collided with his brother.

"Sorry," he mumbled and stepped around him and back into the sultry sun.

Terry's footsteps followed. "Bro, chill." He grabbed Caden's arm.

Caden faced him. "What?"

"I'm worried about you. That's all."

He released a breath. If the situation was reversed, he'd likely feel the same. But that was only because Terry didn't know Stephanie. "I just don't want her to receive the first degree or cold shoulder when she arrives."

Terry raised his hands, palms out. "She won't get any flak from me."

"Okay." While his brother might not have been as accepting as he would've liked, he couldn't fault him for his reaction. He was the oldest, after all, the guy who'd challenged more than one of Caden's bullies growing up.

"Just give her a chance," he said. "That's all I'm asking."

Terry studied him for a moment, but then gave a nod. "Like Pastor Roger said this morning, love expects the best, not the worst, in others. Women stealing my baby brother's heart included."

Caden laughed, trying to think of a comeback. Stephanie's car pulling into the drive averted his thoughts and halted his steps.

Her gaze met his, and his stomach responded similar to how it used to in college speech class. Only not because of dread but rather the anticipation of spending an evening with this woman who'd quickly invaded his thoughts and dreams.

Breaking eye contact, she glanced at Maddy behind her, said something and got out. "Hello." She smiled and moved to the rear passenger door.

By the time Caden reached her, she'd unbuckled Maddy.

"Mistew Caden." She spilled out of the vehicle wearing glittery plastic dress-up shoes and a rainbow tutu over purple polka-dot leggings. "I'm a ballewina. See." Arms out, she twirled in a circle.

He chuckled. "That you are."

Stephanie approached carrying the child's sandals. "I tried to explain why her 'fancy shoes' weren't appropriate for horse riding, but she insisted this was indeed proper attire for all 'princesses,' which obviously, she is."

"Obviously." He ascended the porch stairs ahead of them, then with a bow, he opened the door. "After you, Your Highness."

Maddy giggled, then raising her chin, led the way inside.

The house, as noisy and busy as normal for a Sunday evening, smelled of cheesy potatoes and herb-roasted beef. He proceeded into the dining room.

"Just in time." Mom set a large salad bowl in the center

of the table. "Caden, would you slice the meat? Stephanie, mind grabbing the dressings from the fridge?"

"Yes, ma'am," they said in unison.

His mom seemed to like Stephanie, and he found himself imagining future evenings just like this. Thanksgivings and Christmases.

He was getting way ahead of himself. "I'll grab the milk." He darted around his nephew, who'd sneaked in hoping to snatch a roll from the basket, and opened the fridge.

"Uh-uh." His mom lifted the rolls above the child's head and followed Stephanie into the dining room.

Once the food had been brought out, his dad arrived, and everyone found their places. Maddy fit right in and immediately began chattering with one of Caden's nieces. His mom appeared quite pleased with the whole arrangement, and to his relief, Terry was warm and conversational.

In fact, by the time dinner was finished, he'd almost seemed to warm up to Stephanie. He, along with everyone else, had certainly taken to cute little Maddy.

"Howsies?" She tried to wiggle out of her booster.

"Absolutely." Caden took one last swig of sweet tea and stood. "As soon as we clean up."

Stephanie rose to help.

"We've got this." His mom started clearing plates from the table. "Y'all should go before it gets too late."

"Are you sure?" While he wasn't one to shirk his duties, there was no way he could send Stephanie and Maddy home a second time without their promised ride.

"Don't go arguing with your mama, now." The twinkle in his dad's eye belied his firm tone.

Caden laughed. "Alright." He lowered to Maddy's level. "You ready to go ride some horses?"

"Yes." Grinning wide, she bounced in place and started chanting, "Howsies. Howsies. Howsies." She kept chanting all the way to the stables, skipping ahead while Caden and Stephanie followed a few paces behind.

The breeze stirred Stephanie's hair, and she tucked it behind her ear. "Your parents are so precious together. It's obvious they love each other deeply."

"That they do." They had the type of marriage he hoped to have one day. He'd begun to think maybe that wasn't in his future, that he'd never find a woman who would touch his heart the way his mom still touched his father's.

Then he'd met Stephanie.

She was everything he wanted in a woman. Smart, hard-working, compassionate.

If only he could put his questions regarding her past, regarding the drugs, behind him for good. While his heart assured him she wasn't involved, the smallest fraction of his brain wasn't as certain.

Lord, give me wisdom. I want to do right by You, by her, by the clinic.

After Renée, he'd promised to never let a woman shatter his heart again. And here he was, falling hard for another woman, hoping, praying Stephanie would be different.

He paused outside the stables to scoop grain from the barrels flanking the entrance. He poured some in Maddy's hands. "You got it?"

With the seriousness of one holding a fistful of gems, she nodded.

He looked at Stephanie, delighted by the pure joy that radiated from her eyes as she watched her daughter. "How about you?"

"I'm okay, but thank you."

"You sure?"

She laughed. "If you insist."

He loved seeing her almost childlike side poke through as she opened her hands, palms up. It was all he could do not to pull her to him and kiss her right then and there.

With a cough, he deposited the scooper back in the barrel and led the way to the first stall, belonging to Jasmine, their oldest horse.

"You ready, peanut?" He picked Maddy up, light and sweet as the box of honey he'd carried earlier, so that she could reach. "Hold your hand flat, like this." He demonstrated.

She copied him, squealing when Jasmine's feathery lips scooped up the grain.

"Mowe, pwease?"

"You can have mine." Stephanie's eyes sparkled with laughter. Leaning close enough that he could smell her sweet shampoo and feel the ends of her silky hair against his forearm, she poured her grain into her daughter's hands.

He could've stayed like that, with Maddy in his arms and Stephanie at his side, for the rest of the night, but after a few minutes, Maddy grew restless.

"Looks like someone's ready for that horse ride I promised." He smoothed his hand over her hair.

"Yeah!" She jumped up and down.

He laughed. "I'll be right back." He traipsed off to the tack room to grab the riding gear.

Ten minutes later, they'd strapped a saddle on Kit Kat and a helmet on Maddy, and Caden was leading them both around the arena. The child beamed with joy.

The same joy he saw in Stephanie as she leaned against the fence, watching them. Seeing her standing there, framed by the sun, hair blowing gently in the wind, about took his breath away.

"Thank you." Moisture shimmered in her eyes.

"It's my pleasure." And truly, it was. He couldn't think of a better way to spend his evening than with these two ladies who had managed to capture him so completely. Who'd had him rethinking his whole life, if he were honest.

Reconsidering dreams he'd let die when his former fiancée left him with a broken heart and an empty pocketbook.

Maybe marriage and a family were in his future after all. But what about his clinic? Could he manage both?

He'd just have to figure it out, because some things were worth fighting for.

Chapter Fifteen

Monday morning, Stephanie tried to focus on her patients, but her mind kept drifting to Caden, dinner at his family's and the dance the night before that. She'd felt such hope, and still did, that she might actually experience real love.

Maybe one day her daughter would have a daddy.

"Should I be concerned, Ms. Thornton?"

Her client's worried voice jolted Stephanie back to the present. She offered her most reassuring smile. "Most likely Ace just has a stomach bug." She was about to say Caden would be in shortly when the exam room door behind her opened.

He entered looking slightly tense. "Mrs. Baird." He crossed the room to shake her hand, then petted the pug-bulldog mix panting on her lap. "Hello, there, Ace, buddy. I hear you're not feeling well."

Mrs. Baird repeated what she'd told Stephanie.

"Let's take a look, but first, can you excuse Ms. Thornton and me for a moment?"

"Yes, of course," she said.

He motioned toward the door, and his expression seemed almost sad, or maybe apologetic.

Had something happened? They were probably getting

behind on appointments, as usual, and he wanted her to examine another patient while he took care of Ace.

"Of course." She followed him into the hall.

"Sheriff Talbert is here, and he'd like to speak with you."

Her lungs squeezed, making her feel light-headed. A sheriff? Here? To see her? Had John been released? Was she in danger?

Had something happened to Maddy? She struggled for air, her breaths short and quick. She needed to call the Herrons.

Caden placed a hand on her arm, making her jump. "It's okay. You're okay." He rubbed her back, his voice low. Soothing. "He just wants to talk. About the clinic."

She nodded and focused on her breathing. In through her nose, out through her mouth. *I'm fine. Everything is okay. Maddy's okay.*

"Did you need a minute?" His brow furrowed, his hand still warm on her back. "Some water?"

"Yes. Please."

While he darted off to the break room, she leaned against the wall, her heart racing so fast her chest hurt. *Calm down.* She reviewed the steps her therapists had given her for dealing with panic attacks. *Close my eyes. Breathe deep and slow. In through my nose, out through my mouth. Find something to focus on.*

She opened her eyes and centered her gaze on the dishes in the sink. Two mugs. One brown, one white. A half empty soap dispenser.

She thought back to her first day at college, when she'd thought she'd seen her ex-husband. From a distance, the man standing with his back to her had looked like him. Same height, build, dressed similar to what her ex often wore. But then he turned around.

She hadn't been able to breathe normally for nearly ten minutes. She'd felt as foolish then as she did now.

Caden returned with a glass of water, looking just as concerned as when he'd left. "How can I help?"

She smoothed her hair from her face. "I'm good. I'm sorry about that. I just—"

He pressed a finger to her lips. "Shh. You don't have to explain." His eyes searched hers, his gaze intense, and for a moment, it was as if they were locked in time. But then he blinked and took half a step back. "Sheriff Talbert is in the break room. I told him you'd be in shortly. Want me to walk you back?"

Such a sweet gesture, but she needed to act like the grown woman she was. "I'm fine. You attend to Ace."

"Oh. Right." He gave a soft laugh, lingered for a moment.

She turned and walked away. Why would the police come here? Was this regarding Dr. Wallow's death in some way? She'd been reading too many suspense novels. She almost laughed out loud.

The sheriff sat at the break room table, reviewing whatever he'd written on his pocket notepad. Papers lay spread before him.

He stood when Stephanie entered. "Mrs. Thornton." He shook her hand, then motioned to the chair across from him. "Please, have a seat."

She complied.

"Did Dr. Stoughton tell you why I'm here?"

She shook her head.

"Your ex-husband likes to party, doesn't he?"

So this *was* about John. She wrapped her arms around herself and nodded. "He had a drug and alcohol problem." She assumed he'd had plenty of time to clean up while behind bars. Though she wouldn't be surprised if he fell right back into drinking and drugging once he got out.

"Did you share his habit?"

"What?" She blinked. What was this about? What had

John done? Whatever it was, surely the authorities couldn't think she was involved. "No. Of course not."

"But he shared, right? Gave you a hit every once in a while? That's why you joined that Next Steps program in California?"

"No, sir."

"Have you ever taken controlled substances that weren't doctor prescribed?"

"No, sir."

"Are any of your friends involved in drugs?"

"Honestly, I'm pretty new here. I haven't made many friends, other than the Herrons. And Cad—Dr. Stoughton."

"How are you doing financially?"

Was he interrogating her? Did he think she'd stolen something? Drugs? Preposterous.

She swallowed. "I don't need for much. The Herrons let me stay with them and eat their food free of charge. And they watch my daughter, so I don't have to pay for day care."

"Someone's been stealing clinic narcotics. You got any idea who that somebody could be?"

"What?" She blinked against the sting of tears. "I have no idea."

As he continued asking questions, his gaze became more pointed, as if he didn't believe her answers. He obviously suspected her. And why wouldn't he? She was the newbie, the outsider. Of course she'd be the first person he suspected. What if, in a rush to solve his case, he pinned the theft on her? She didn't have money for a lawyer. What if failure to secure adequate defense landed her in jail?

Did Caden suspect her, too? And if not now, would he?

That would completely shatter her heart.

By the time the sheriff excused her, she felt sick to her stomach and on the verge of tears. She wanted to believe truth would win out, but life had taught her that wasn't always the case. John had punished her for plenty she'd never even considered doing.

What if the real culprit found a way to pin the theft on her? She'd certainly had access, with all the time she'd spent doing inventory.

Upon Caden's request. What if he'd taken the narcotics and had seen her as a perfect scapegoat? What if what she'd attributed to fatigue, stress and discouragement had actually been signs of drug use?

No. He wasn't the type. He was loyal, honest, hardworking…

She'd once thought the same about John.

She felt light-headed and queasy.

Hurrying out of the break room, she headed toward the staff bathroom to splash some water on her face but halted mid-step. Caden and the sheriff were standing outside his office. Upon seeing her, they abruptly stopped talking, and Caden's expression looked conflicted, almost hurt.

Or remorseful?

Lungs tight, she took in a deep breath and pushed into the bathroom, closed the door and leaned against it. If she got arrested, what would happen to Maddy? She closed her eyes to keep from crying.

God, I need Your help. If not for me, then for Maddy. Please.

Her phone rang, making her jump. She glanced at the screen. Cassandra. "Hello?"

"Hey, sugar-pie. Everything alright? Your voice sounds croakier than a tree frog strung up by his toes."

She worried if she spoke, she'd burst out in tears.

"What is it?" Casandra's voice was gentle.

"Nothing." She didn't want to talk about it.

What if Cassandra assumed that Stephanie must be guilty for the officer to question her in the first place? Not to mention, Cassandra had more history with everyone else connected with the clinic than she had with Stephanie. She knew them better. If it came down to her word against Caden's, or Lisa's, or any other Sage Creek resident for that matter, Stephanie's claims of innocence might not carry much weight.

Hopefully Cassandra knew her better than that. But her experience with her ex-husband had taught her that people could become suspicious with little provocation.

Cassandra isn't John. She exhaled. "It's been a stressful day, is all."

"Sounds like you could use a hilarious night out with the girls."

"What?"

"Remember that painting event I told you about? I sort of forgot all about it, but, well, it's tonight."

"Oh." That was the last thing Stephanie wanted to do this evening. "I'm not sure—"

"It'll be fun. Promise."

"What about Maddy?"

"Lucy offered to take her. She's got to watch a couple of grandkids anyway. Way I figure it, this will provide an opportunity for you and your little one to make friends."

Stephanie would much rather spend the night in bed, with the blankets pulled over her head.

"Come on, girl," Cassandra said. "You can't hide away at the house forever. Folks will start thinking you're antisocial or something."

Though Cassandra's playful tone indicated she was teasing, Stephanie worried she might be right. Isolating herself could increase people's suspicions of her, the sheriff's included.

"Yeah, okay," she said.

"Yeah? Yippee!"

Stephanie could almost envision Cassandra giving a little bounce.

The bathroom door thumped her from behind, and she moved out of the way.

Lisa poked her head through the opening. "Oops. Sorry." She stepped inside, her surprised expression hardening with the same glint of suspicion Stephanie had seen in the sheriff's eyes.

"I've got to go." Stephanie rubbed the back of her arm.

"Of course." Cassandra clanked dishes in the background over the sound of Maddy's chirping voice. "I was just about to break out Play-Doh, anyway. I best get to it before this precious little one of yours loses her patience."

Lisa continued eyeing Stephanie as she hung up and slipped her phone into her scrubs shirt pocket. "Important call?"

"Not really."

"But you had to come into the bathroom to make it."

"No. I was just…" What was she implying? "That was Mrs. Herron, inviting me to something." While she absolutely didn't owe Lisa an explanation, neither would it help to withhold it.

Lisa pursed her lips. "I see."

Was this what Stephanie would experience from here on out? So much for assuming the best in others. Then again, she didn't expect much different from Lisa. The woman had disliked her from day one.

Because she was the thief? That would explain why she always acted so territorial.

"Excuse me." Stephanie stepped around her and out into the hall, doing her best to focus on their remaining appointments.

Unfortunately, not even her encounter with an adorable and highly energetic pug could soothe her nerves. As a result, by the time she arrived at the painting party, an activity she would've already found draining, she felt emotionally exhausted and had developed a tension headache.

Cassandra cut the car engine and shifted to face her. "The acetaminophen kicking in yet?"

Stephanie inhaled and nodded. "Thanks." She studied the two-story brick home kitty-corner from where they'd parked.

Bushes lined the length of the house, and cheery yellow bells interspersed with daisies decorated both sides of the walk. Based on the vehicles spilling from the driveway and into the street, they were among the last to arrive.

"These gals are going to love you, trust me." Cassandra patted her leg. "You have nothing to be ashamed of or any reason to feel inferior. You know that, right? In fact, I'm pretty sure if they knew your story, all you've overcome, they'd be in awe."

Stephanie gave a nervous laugh. "I'm not so sure about that." Especially if rumors had started swirling regarding the drug theft and her conversation with the sheriff.

"Well, I am." She grinned. "Your social anxiety is normal, considering. But you'll get your confidence back. Bit by bit. You've come a long way, and you should be proud of that. But you still have a ways to go. That means you need to march on into that house with your head high, eat all the chocolate your stomach can hold and rediscover how to enjoy yourself. To have fun for fun's sake."

Her shoulders relaxed some. "You're right." While she might always bear scars from her ex-husband's abuse, her life *had* changed for the better. She was relearning how to rest, to laugh. And how to love. And she wouldn't let misguided suspicions, or even false accusations, if it came to that, steal the progress she'd made.

She thought of the peach festival she'd be attending in a couple days—with Caden. Yesterday, she'd been thinking about what a gift he'd been to her. How patient, and compassionate in a way that made her feel stronger.

But now? What if he believed she took the drugs? How would he treat her then?

"How about we pray right quick?" Cassandra asked.

Stephanie released a breath. "I would love that."

She closed her eyes, mentally adding to Cassandra's request. She asked God to protect her and Maddy, to guide the investigation and to help her trust that He would. God had done so much already. She saw that now. He'd kept Maddy safe in her womb that night John had beaten her. How He'd removed John from her life when she wasn't sure she had the strength and courage to leave. He'd led her to the shelter, where she received help and a chance to start over. Even the fact that she was here now was evidence of God's care.

She chose to believe He'd stay with her. That He wouldn't bring her this far to let everything fall apart.

Cassandra grabbed her purse from behind her seat. "We best get before those gals eat up all that chocolate." She winked and got out.

She waited on the sidewalk for Stephanie to join her, then linked arms as they approached the stoop.

A short blonde woman Stephanie recognized from church answered the door. "Mrs. Herron, hello." She gave Cassandra a hug, then smiled at Stephanie. "Hi. Stephanie, right?" Her wide grin matched her friendly brown eyes.

She nodded and glanced past her to the women gathered in her living room and beyond. Only about half of them looked familiar, though she didn't really know any of them.

"I'm Mallory." The host moved aside. "Come on in and grab yourself a glass of sweet tea. We'll start painting soon."

"Thanks." Stephanie stepped into the dim interior, and she and Cassandra were immediately engulfed in laughter and chatter.

Stephanie's eyes widened. The owner of the mobile vet

was here. She stood across the room, talking with an older woman with short curly hair. Something made her laugh, and she shifted, her gaze sweeping the width of the room before landing on Stephanie.

Renée smiled and waved.

Stephanie nodded a greeting in response. Her curiosity made her want to get to know Renée better. To learn why Caden disliked her so. While he never said anything, he clearly felt animosity toward her.

"Come on." Cassandra patted her arm. "I'll introduce you to folks." She led her to three ladies of varying sizes and ages gathered near a stone fireplace. They were immediately pulled into a conversation centered on watercolors and acrylics. Most everyone, it seemed, had attended numerous "painting parties" as they called them. Apparently, that was one of the perks of having a local artist in town who received joy sharing her passion with others.

"She's legit." A tall brunette grabbed a handful of chocolate-covered almonds from a nearby dish. "She used to sell her work in a gallery in Austin. I think she might still have some pieces on display. But when a fire nearly destroyed our church, she came to restore the stained-glass windows, met her true love and well, here she is." She swept both arms wide.

"Alright, y'all." A woman with long, brown wavy hair emerged from the kitchen carrying a stack of canvases. She wore a paint-splattered apron. "Quit making me sound like a female Monet." She faced Stephanie. "I'm Faith, the person tasked with corralling this group into the kitchen. Preferably *before* y'all's paint dries."

She started ushering everyone toward a long rectangular table covered with newspaper. She'd placed various painting supplies in front of each chair.

Sitting between Cassandra and their host, Stephanie did her best to keep all the names straight. Everyone seemed so friendly, like women she might want to connect with. And if their smiles and cheerful tones were any indication, they even seemed open to the idea.

Either these women hadn't heard about the sheriff's visit to the clinic or didn't care.

Faith moved her easel to a location where all could easily see. "This is what we'll be painting." She held up an acrylic of three coneflowers on a swirled, marbleized background. "We'll begin with the background, using a pour technique. Grab a plastic cup from the stack in front of you, and add a bit of paint, maybe four drops, of each of these colors—without mixing them. White, double the amount of blue, purple, a small drop of black."

Cassandra smiled. "My favorite type of flower."

Faith laughed. "I would think so. How's your crop doing?"

"Very well, thank you." She grabbed a container of light blue paint. "We'll sell tea at the peach festival and will harvest the roots this fall."

"Wait." Renée paused with a cup in one hand and a jug of white paint in the other. "You have an echinacea farm?"

Cassandra nodded. "First year, but yes. I've devoted an acre of land east of our orchards. The coneflowers were growing on their own. When I learned that's where echinacea comes from, I figured we might as well turn them into a profit."

Renée smiled. "I would love to buy some of your roots. I've been experimenting with more naturopathic treatments."

"Sure." Cassandra looked at Stephanie. "Maybe you should take some to the clinic, too. See if Caden has any interest in trying holistic veterinary medicine."

"I can ask," Stephanie said.

"So." The woman to her left nudged her. "What's it like working with the most eligible bachelor in Sage Creek?"

She had short blond hair and wore bright orangish-red lipstick. "I hear you two might have a thing going."

Stephanie nearly choked on her sweet tea.

"Heidi," Mallory exclaimed.

"What? A woman can ask, can't she?"

Stephanie's face felt ready to combust.

Before she could respond, an older woman at the end of the table said, "Wait a minute." She studied Stephanie with a frown. "You're that gal from California? The one causing problems for that poor Stoughton boy?"

An awkward silence filled the kitchen.

Stephanie blinked. "What?"

"Hillary, how in the world could you say such a thing?" Faith crossed her arms. "She's *helping* him, and during a time when he seriously needs it."

"Is she now?" Hillary raised an eyebrow. "Then tell me, dear, who do you think stole those drugs? You for sure know it wasn't Lisa. Or Paul for that matter. Who else is there?"

"That's for Sheriff Talbert and his crew to figure out." Cassandra's voice carried a definite edge.

The woman huffed. "One certainly hopes. Before she destroys Caden's credibility. Not to mention Dr. Wallow's legacy. If he only knew."

Stephanie felt sick. Was that how people saw her?

Were they saying such things to Caden, as well? Was she hurting his business by creating distrust? And what about when people saw her standing beside him at the booth on Wednesday? How many others shared Hillary's suspicions and would feel a need to "express" their concerns?

She'd been so looking forward to that night.

Until now.

Though the rest of the evening went well, and most of the women seemed intent on making Stephanie feel welcome, she struggled to shake off her insecurities.

When she got up to refill her sweet tea, Cassandra met her in the kitchen.

She placed a hand on Stephanie's shoulder. "Don't let the words of one woman tear you down."

She nodded. She'd dealt with—and overcome—a lot more than snarky comments at a social gathering. And as to the drug theft, she had nothing to hide.

The truth would come out. She chose to believe that.

Chapter Sixteen

The next evening, after a tense and uncomfortable work-day, Stephanie arrived home feeling frazzled and increasingly insecure. Caden had been kind, and of course he would be. She could tell he wanted to trust her, but also that he didn't. The fact that his suspicion stung as much as it did demonstrated how important he'd become to her.

She'd fallen for him.

The teakettle on the stove whistled. "You know what you need?" Cassandra grabbed a mug. "Fresh air and ice cream."

"Ice cweem?" Maddy, building blocks on the floor, peered up at Stephanie with big hope-filled eyes.

Stephanie laughed. "That sounds fun." Sitting around fretting wouldn't help any. Although with her future so uncertain, junk food wasn't the best use of her money.

"My treat."

As usual, Cassandra sensed Stephanie's challenge without her having to say a thing. "You don't have to do that."

"I want to. I could use the stress reliever, and chasing after little sweet pea sure would provide that. Way I figure it, you'd be doing me a favor. Things will turn busy enough come Wednesday. Might as well take advantage of tonight. Get us some girl time while we can, isn't that right,

Maddy?" She gave her ponytail a playful tug. "Speaking of—remember Ms. Lucy from church?"

Stephanie nodded.

"She said she'd love to spend time with our princess during the festival. If that's alright with you."

"Absolutely." She trusted Cassandra's judgment implicitly.

"Great." She returned her mug to the cupboard. "Now, let's grab us something sweet and head to the park. Might as well drop off some coneflower roots to Renée on our way back. Give me a minute to grab some for her."

She dashed off, returning a short time later with two lumpy plastic bags.

The entire drive into town, Maddy alternated between singing songs she must've learned during Sunday school and asking questions about everything from why the sky was blue to how many babies mama butterflies had.

Her enthusiasm increased tenfold once they reached Dreamy Creamery, the local ice cream shop. The moment they walked in, Maddy yanked free of Stephanie's hand and dashed to the display counter. Face pressed to the glass, hands on either side of her head, she gazed at the different flavors.

Cassandra chuckled. "I'd say someone's excited."

Stephanie smiled, touched to know her daughter had something of a surrogate grandmother in the older woman.

Maddy chose a scoop of strawberry, covered with sprinkles. Stephanie chose chocolate mint, and Cassandra selected a waffle cone with a scoop of blueberry swirl and another of fudge brownie.

She grabbed some napkins and placed a hand on the back of Maddy's head. "Think you can eat and walk, sweet pea?"

Tip of her nose dabbed with ice cream, she nodded.

Cassandra tucked her change in her pocket. "You good with that, Mama? The park's about five blocks away."

"Sounds lovely."

Taking Maddy's free hand, Cassandra led them out. Thanks to a light cloud cover and a steady breeze, the temperature felt pleasant. Someone honked. Stephanie glanced up to see a woman she vaguely remembered from church waving enthusiastically at Cassandra.

Stephanie could get used to living in a town like this, where people knew your name and acted like they actually cared to know your story. Where nearly wherever you went, you were practically guaranteed to run into a friendly face.

She thought of the angry woman from the night before and frowned.

Or a not-so-friendly face. Hopefully she was the exception.

They continued past the library and the boutique Caden had taken her to in preparation for their first date, which hadn't been a date but sure felt like one.

Where would things sit with them now, with all this suspicion surrounding her?

The town park was an expanse of dandelion and clover-dotted grass. Tall trees cast shadowed patches across the landscape, and birds chirped among their knotted branches.

Across the way, a younger couple leaned, shoulder to shoulder, against a large tree trunk. Another couple, maybe twenty years older, occupied one of three benches placed along a winding bike path. Fifty or so yards to their left, a teen with short red hair sprawled on her stomach reading a book.

Maddy darted off toward a metal turtle stuck in the sand while Stephanie and Cassandra sat on a nearby bench.

"You've been pretty quiet regarding that whole drug theft mess." Cassandra licked melting ice cream off her cone. "Want to talk about it?"

Stephanie relayed what had happened.

"Poor kid's sure got a lot to deal with. Guess all we can do is pray for him and the clinic."

"Maybe me, as well." She shared her concerns.

"You don't have to worry about that." Cassandra patted her hand. "Sheriff Talbert is as honest, true and capable as they come. He won't go wherever his investigation doesn't lead him. 'Course..." She studied Stephanie. "That's assuming you had nothing to do with all that garbage?"

Stephanie's stomach sank. "Of course not." How could Cassandra even ask such a thing?

"Figured as much." She gave her hand a squeeze. "This'll blow over soon enough. Always does."

Before or after Caden lost his practice?

A child jumped off the swing, and Maddy scampered to take his place. "Mama, help me?"

Stephanie and Cassandra stood, almost in unison, and walked to the swings, Cassandra lingering near the metal pole while Stephanie pushed.

"Look who's here." Cassandra pointed.

Stephanie followed her line of sight to where Renée's mobile vet parked. Was she here seeing patients?

"Too bad I left the coneflower roots in the car." Cassandra wiped her glistening forehead with the back of her hand.

"I can go get them." Seemed the least she could do, considering Cassandra's kindness to her and Maddy.

"You sure?"

"Absolutely. The walk will give me time to think." Maybe the brisk movement would eat up some of her nervous energy.

"Thank you." Cassandra handed over her keys.

Stephanie took them and hurried off, returning ten minutes later with bags in hand and slightly out of breath. But the exercise had felt good.

She approached the mobile vet, then lingered near the door. Should she knock? Was Renée here? Did she make house calls?

Stephanie eyed the homes across the street.

She was just about to leave when Renée emerged from her van with a gawky goldendoodle and a short bald man.

"Enjoy your evening." She smiled and, giving Stephanie a quick nod in greeting, scratched the dog behind the ears.

Once the patient and owner left, she faced Stephanie. "Hello."

"Ma'am." While she felt bad for not calling, she'd never promised she would. As much as she needed a job, she hadn't decided how she'd feel about working for Caden's competition, who, according to Cassandra, was also his ex-girlfriend. How he'd feel were she to do so.

"This is from Mrs. Herron." She gave her the bags of roots.

Renée peered inside. "Perfect, thank you." She paused. "You still looking for work?"

Stephanie studied her, knowing precisely where this conversation would lead, should she answer honestly. Truth was, she needed a job, and with all the suspicion surrounding Caden's clinic... What if the DEA shut his place down? Or he lost his license? That could happen, couldn't it?

A gust of wind swirled her hair around her head. She held it back with her forearm. "Sort of, yes."

"I heard about the open drug case. I imagine that's quite unsettling and leads to a lot of uncertainty."

Her statement reignited Stephanie's anxiety. Should she be discussing the issue with her? "I assume business has been going well?"

"Almost too well, you might say. I'd love to continue the conversation we began at the grain and feed store."

Stephanie chewed her bottom lip and gazed toward the

playground. Catching Cassandra's eye, Stephanie shot her a short text.

She quickly replied, encouraging her to speak with Renée. Three additional texts followed: Listen. Learn. Open mind.

Stephanie exhaled. She could do that. Besides, who knew how God might lead? As a single mom, she wasn't in a position to close any doors He might be opening.

If Dr. Elkins offered her a job, Stephanie would simply have to trust God to work things out between her and Caden. Or make it clear she wasn't to accept the offer. Wasn't that what the Herrons always told her—to focus on following God and leave everything else, other people's reactions included, to Him?

She smiled. "Sure. I can chat for a moment."

At this point, it was just a conversation. No harm could come from that. She'd worry about the rest when it came time.

"Let's step out of the sun for a minute and slip into my fancy little office." Renée motioned toward her vet mobile.

Stephanie offered a nervous smile and followed her into the much cooler vehicle.

Renée had converted the inside into something like an exam room. A counter and sink lined one wall, with a counter holding a scale, microscope and additional items along the other. The space smelled like an oddly comforting mixture of dog and antiseptic that reminded her of college labs.

"This is where the magic happens and drama unfolds." Renée laughed. "I average about ten appointments a day, mostly well-pet visits and the occasional stomach upset. As you can see, I'm not equipped to handle anything major."

Then she'd never truly be a threat to Caden. Maybe the two could even work together. "Do you refer patients needing surgery out?"

"Pretty much."

"Have you approached Caden?"

She frowned and dropped her gaze. "I'm not sure he'd go for that."

Once again, Stephanie wondered what had caused such animosity between them. All of their reactions—Caden's, Lisa's and Renée's—suggested something more than competition.

That really wasn't her business. Maybe if she got hired on, and that was a big if, she could broach the subject. Act like something of a bridge between the two. Seemed they could help each other out.

"Have you interviewed anyone else?" Stephanie asked.

"No one I'm crazy about."

"Any chance you'll ever open an office?"

"Maybe. Although I like how things are now. My flexibility, mobility, low overhead. Either way, my business is growing, and I'd love for you to come on board and grow with me."

It felt good to know she had options, should Caden decide not to hire her. Despite the disappointment she'd feel, were that to occur, she had to believe it would be because he didn't have the funds.

What would working for Dr. Elkins do to their relationship?

She worried circumstances might force her to choose between the man she loved and caring for Maddy. Regardless, she needed to support her daughter.

Caden sat on his porch steps and picked up a well-chewed and soggy stick. "You ready, boy?" He waved it in front of Rocky, then tossed it as far as he could. The dog darted off and soon returned, ready for another round.

Caden glanced toward Bella, lying in the house's shade. The gray in her muzzle and around her eyes revealed her age. "Not interested in joining, huh?"

She'd slowed down significantly over the past year. Caden hated to think what that meant.

He grabbed the stick Rocky had once again deposited in front of him and threw it even farther than the first time.

Had Sheriff Talbert uncovered anything today? He'd said he and his team were going through clinic staff's financials. How long would that take? And how far would rumors run in the meantime?

There was no way this could involve anyone from his staff. But who else could it be? What if they never figured that out? That happened. Some cases were never solved.

Would suspicion hang over Caden's head indefinitely? Maybe even cost him the clinic?

He refused to believe that could happen.

The distant hum of an engine turned his attention to the dirt road leading onto his property. Looked to be his brother's truck, kicking up a swirl of dust in his wake.

Odd he'd be coming out here on a Monday, especially considering Caden had just seen him the night before. Had something happened to Mama or Dad? Or one of their siblings? He checked his phone. No missed texts or calls.

Chest tight, he stood and waited, the air suddenly thick and heavy.

Terry parked in front of Caden's house and stepped out of his truck. "Got a minute?"

He recognized the stern look on his brother's face. Whatever had brought him here, it wasn't for a social call.

"I was just hanging with my dogs." He motioned toward Rocky, who stood before him, clutching his slobbery stick in his mouth. "You want to come in for a spell?"

Terry studied him for a minute, then gave one quick nod.

Caden led the way into his house, the dim interior almost blinding in contrast to the bright summer sun. "Coffee or tea?" He took off his cowboy hat and set it on the short

Formica breakfast counter their dad helped him install. A stack of mail he hadn't had time to go through lay beside it.

"Dude. It's five hundred degrees out." Terry plopped onto the couch.

"Good point." He went into the kitchen and returned with two tall glasses of sweet tea and extra ice. "Haven't thought a lick about supper, but I've got some chicken nuggets in the freezer. Want me to nuke you some?"

"The missus has a casserole in the oven."

In other words, this would be a short visit. Definitely not a social call.

He set his drink on the coffee table and sat in his worn and sun-bleached recliner. "What's up?"

"This is about Stephanie."

Caden tensed. "Look, I know you're worried. With all that's going on at the clinic, I understand your concern." Why were they having this conversation again? Unless Terry had heard something from Sheriff Talbert. Those two were friends. Still, Caden would've expected the sheriff would talk to him if anything came to light.

An image of Stephanie standing in the clinic hall, nearly hyperventilating, came to mind. What if the officer had read her reaction for guilt? Granted, she'd seemed to calm down considerably before heading to the break room, but she'd still acted nervous. Jumpy. Sheriff Talbert had joked more than once about "telltale guilty behavior." He said, in his experience, criminals' body language gave them away long before they opened their mouths.

Was that how he viewed Stephanie?

Bigger question—did Caden have a blind spot when it came to her?

"I say this with the utmost love and respect," Caden said. "It's not your concern who I do or do not date."

"You two are officially dating, then?"

"I didn't say that. What I did say, however, was to mind your own business."

Jaw tight, Caden waited for Terry to throw his broken engagement in his face. To remind him of his poor judgment when it came to women. But Caden had wised up since then. Heartache had a way of maturing a person. Or making them bitter, but praise God, He'd helped Caden choose the former.

Terry sighed. "I don't care to meddle with your love life. I just came to relay some facts."

"I don't know what you heard or think you heard, but you should know better than—"

"It's what I saw."

Caden's stomach dipped. Saw what? Stephanie stealing? Or out around town acting strange, like she was on something? No. Whatever Terry thought he'd seen, he was mistaken.

Caden took in a deep breath. "I'm listening."

Terry went on to tell him about an interaction he'd witnessed between Stephanie and the mobile vet. "You said Renée was offering clients unsustainably low rates. Free drugs could account for that."

"That doesn't make sense. Why would Stephanie steal from me and give the meds to Renée?"

"Money."

"She wouldn't."

"Then who?"

Caden didn't have an answer for that.

And if it was Stephanie? That'd shred his heart, because as much as he'd tried to fight against it, he'd fallen for her. He knew that now. The thought of finding out she wasn't who he thought left a hollow ache in his chest.

Chapter Seventeen

The next morning, Caden asked Stephanie to speak with him privately in his office. She was obviously nervous. From guilt or the weight of suspicion? He wanted to believe she reacted from the latter, and he could certainly understand that. But he needed to hear that from her. For her to look him in the eye as she said it.

"Have a seat."

She perched on the edge of her chair while he rounded his desk and sat behind it. He studied her for a moment, trying to formulate his thoughts and to make sense of his confusing, conflicting emotions. He feared he'd lost all objectivity.

"How do you know Renée Elkins?" he asked.

She picked at a cuticle, one of her telltale nervous signs. "I ran into her at the feed supply store." She went on to explain their interaction.

"What's your relationship with her now?"

"I can't say that we really have one. Like I mentioned previously, my first preference would be to work here, for you. But…"

"But?"

"I have to provide for Maddy."

"What are you saying?" She was a mom. A mom would

do whatever necessary to care for her daughter. That had always been clear. But would that involve stealing narcotics? "What did you bring her yesterday?"

"I'm sorry?"

"What was in the plastic bag that you handed her?"

Her face seemed to pale—as if guilty and caught. She blinked a few times and appeared to be fighting tears. "Were you spying on me?" Her tone tightened.

"Should I be?"

"I need to go." She stood and took a couple backward steps toward the door. "Excuse me."

Stunned, he watched her leave. Her reaction could indicate guilt or pain caused by his suspicion. Either way, chasing her down to press her further wouldn't help. He needed to let law enforcement handle this.

His phone chimed an appointment notification, startling him. He checked the time. He needed to visit an alpaca farm owned by a slightly eccentric woman he'd met at the barn dance.

She'd mentioned wanting to find a new vet, but hadn't seemed in a hurry. Not until her voice mail.

One of her females was in trouble. It sounded neurological. While he didn't have extensive experience with the animals, he'd worked with them a time or two.

Lisa popped her head into his office as he was gathering his things. "Stephanie just left. She seemed pretty shook up. Is everything alright?"

Not knowing what to say, he released a heavy breath, shook his head, and walked past her and into the hall.

Lisa followed half a step behind. "What about the festival tomorrow? Need me to fill in for her?"

Right. The festival, when he and Stephanie were supposed to man the clinic booth together. He paused at Lisa's desk. "I can handle it, but thank you." He rubbed the back of his neck. "Dr. Jones should be in any moment to cover things in here."

"I thought he was only going to work on weekends."

"Initially, but his grandfather's health is rapidly declining, so Jones decided to move to Sage Creek." He'd said he wanted to stay close and help with finances. That had to be a heavy burden—his grief compounded with financial stress. Caden understood much too well. While he had not been blood related, Wallow had been pretty close to kin.

Caden felt a bit guilty, gaining such benefit from Dr. Jones's situation, but he hoped to convince him to join the staff full time. Folks had a tendency to grow attached to this community.

He processed all that had happened on his way to the alpaca farm. Stephanie, a drug thief? He still couldn't wrap his mind around that. Nor had he seen her acting suspiciously in the medicine storage area. Sure, she'd had access, and not only when she'd worked through their inventory. He'd also given her the code so she could do so as she had time.

But would she really be so brazen?

With how much she loved Maddy, no. The mom in her would never take such a risk.

But what was in those bags?

Honestly, it could've been anything. Desserts from Mrs. Herron. Something related to the festival. As to the drugs, someone else had taken them. He might not know who that was yet, but he knew for sure it wasn't Stephanie.

He never should have accused her. His words and suspicion had hurt her deeply. It would have him, as well, if the situation had been reversed. He needed to apologize, make things right.

He'd call her as soon as this appointment was over. Hopefully he hadn't destroyed the connection they'd been building. He sensed trust didn't come easily for her and feared his actions might have shattered any he'd built.

Lord, I don't want to lose her. He loved her. He realized that now, more than he'd ever loved a woman.

He turned at a colorful sign announcing Mrs. Ehret's property, then onto a deeply rutted dirt road flanked by tall native grass. As he neared a teal mobile home shaded by a massive old pecan tree, grass gave way to lush pastureland dotted by white, beige and black alpacas.

He parked behind an old green truck with a wide wooden bed occupying most of the drive and cut the engine.

He stepped out of the vehicle to see Mrs. Ehret walking toward him from the east. She wore pink biking shorts, a matching tank top and a visor over her ponytailed hair.

"Dr. Stoughton." She shook his hand. "I appreciate you coming on such short notice. I hope it wasn't too much trouble."

"Not at all, ma'am. I was heading this way to check on some ranching clients anyway. This is beautiful land."

"Thanks." She turned toward a three-sided shed and motioned for him to follow. "Vera's this way."

"Vera?"

"That's my sweet girl's name. It means faith. She was the first alpaca I purchased, my leap of faith, as it were."

"Fitting."

"I thought so, that is, up until now. She's been acting strangely, like she's drunk or something." She led the way into the barn's dark interior, the smell of hay and dirt wafting from the cement floor. "She seems to be growing weaker. I worry she ate something toxic."

Caden examined the animal, asking questions as he did. He suspected tick paralysis. "Can we shear her?"

Less than twenty minutes later, he'd found and removed the tick that confirmed his suspicions. "I'll give her a shot of Ivomec Plus to kill any ticks that might still be attached and antibiotics to keep the bite site from becoming infected. I suggest you give her some sort of tick preventive."

"But she's going to be okay?"

He smiled. "Give her a month, but I expect her to make a full recovery."

Her eyes misted up. "That's such good news. Thank you so much for your help."

"My pleasure." He glanced at his phone. "While I'm here, anything else you need help with?"

"Actually, yes. This is only my second year of raising these sweet creatures, and well, I'm a little uncertain about their nutrition. Would you have time to give me a consultation?"

"Absolutely."

He spent the next fifteen minutes patiently sharing information and answering questions. By the time he left, not only had he earned a new client, but she'd been so thrilled with his visit, she'd promised to shout his praises out to all her friends.

Back in the truck, Caden blasted his air-conditioning and took a long swig from his water bottle. That was a trip well taken.

His phone rang as he was about to turn onto the main road. He glanced at the screen, shifted to Park, then answered. "Sheriff Talbert. Good to hear from you."

"I'm calling to let you know we've solved the drug-theft case."

"Okay." He held his breath.

"A local high school student was admitted to the hospital last night with an overdose. She's going to be okay, praise God. But the whole experience got her talking. She says she got the drugs from Jeff Hollister and that he's been selling to other kids."

He exhaled. Thank goodness it wasn't Stephanie. He knew it couldn't have been her. But…Jeff? How could he?

"Are you sure? The girl could be—"

"Lying? Honestly, I'd hoped that was the case. I really like that Hollister kid. But no. He fessed up this morning."

"Wow. I'm just… Wow. While I'm sorry to hear this, I'm grateful we've finally got answers."

He hung up and deposited his phone on the dash. Then he sat there, staring straight ahead. He was glad his clinic would no longer be under suspicion, and for assurance regarding Stephanie. But Jeff? What could make him do such a thing? He'd shown no signs of drug use or delinquency.

The kid was almost like a little brother to him. And he'd been like a son to Dr. Wallow.

Caden dialed Stephanie's number. It went straight to voice mail. "Hey, it's me. Listen, I want to apologize for questioning you this afternoon." He relayed his conversation with Sheriff Talbert. "I knew it wasn't you. That it couldn't be you." Would she think he was only saying that now because he had proof? If only he'd contacted her before the sheriff had called.

My sweet Stephanie. What pain all this must have caused you. What pain I must've caused you.

Stephanie stood behind the booth Cassandra had allocated for the clinic, waiting for Caden to arrive. She wasn't sure she wanted to see him. She didn't know how to process it all. Honestly, she could understand his initial suspicions. She might've felt the same.

Actually, she had. Maybe she hadn't come right out and questioned him, but she'd wondered briefly if he'd stolen the drugs.

Briefly. That was the difference. She'd known deep in her heart he was much too honorable to be involved in anything so shady. She'd thought he'd known the same about her. But once again, she'd found herself in a relationship with a man who didn't fully trust her.

How much of that was her fault? She hadn't exactly been all that open with him about her past. Except the night of the dance, when she'd told him about the most terrifying period of her life. And he'd been so empathetic. So caring. Like he understood her and her pain.

If only she didn't love him so deeply, then maybe his suspicions wouldn't have hurt her so. But she did love him. More than she'd ever loved John. Actually, her love for Caden had shown her that what she felt for John had never truly been love. Infatuation, maybe. But Caden?

"Hey."

She turned to find Caden and Faith, the woman who'd led the painting party, approaching. He held a large, fragrant bouquet of lavender-and-white flowers.

Decorations for the booth?

Standing straighter, she donned what she hoped to be a confident and professional smile. "Hi. We haven't had many pet owners stop by." Though she had received numerous questions regarding Jeff Hollister and the drug theft. Hopefully, her limited answers appeased people's curiosity—without fueling gossip—so that Caden wouldn't have to deal with any more drama than necessary. The poor guy deserved some privacy to process all that had happened. "Most everyone seems to be hanging around the booths with something cold to drink."

"You mean they aren't interested in melted chocolate?" Motioning toward their candy bowl, Caden chuckled.

She laughed. "Not exactly. If you'd like, I could run to Wilma's and get some pitchers of iced sweet tea."

"Actually, I was hoping you'd take a walk with me." Caden gave her the flowers.

She blinked as a jolt shot through her. "What are these for?"

"Can we talk for a minute? Faith here can man the booth."

She swallowed and nodded, then started to gather her things.

Faith placed a hand on her shoulder. "I can keep an eye on your stuff. If you're comfortable with that."

"Sure." It wasn't like she had much of value in her purse anyway. Nor was she pressed for time. Mrs. Herron and Ms. Lucy had invited Maddy to "help them" for the day, an invitation that had clearly made her cutie rather proud of herself. The way she'd jutted her chin and stretched to her full height had reminded Stephanie of the tremendous gift they both had in that sweet woman.

Faith glanced around. "I bet I can even get someone to bring me a cup of water for those flowers. They're much too beautiful to let them go unattended to."

They were quite lovely. A thank-you for helping to man the booth? Or…

She hesitated, the jitters she'd been feeling all morning intensifying. "Thank you." She handed the flowers to Faith, then exited the booth to where Caden stood.

Hand on the small of her back, Caden guided her through the stream of oncoming festival attendees.

At the children's play area, they paused to let a group of children run in front of them. Most of the apparatuses looked handcrafted, likely built by Mr. Herron and some of his church buddies. There were two wooden balance beams, a climbing structure made from old tractor tires and another one with webbing created from thick, intertwining rope.

"Is Maddy enjoying the festival?" Caden asked as they resumed walking.

"She seemed to be last I saw her. Mrs. Herron brought her by the booth to bring me a snow cone. Her face, tongue and hand had been stained blue."

"That had to be adorable."

She smiled at the fact that he hadn't immediately thought of the mess. "She was."

"And nothing that a quick run through the sprinklers the Herrons set up near their strawberry patch can't clean up, I'm sure."

What a day that little peanut would have! This was exactly the type of life she'd long dreamed of for her daughter.

But without Caden, their life would feel incomplete. If only Jeff hadn't stolen the clinic's drugs, then Caden never would've suspected her and her heart wouldn't feel so bruised. So…insecure.

He paused at the brick pavers leading to the Herrons'. "Mind if I swing by your place right quick?"

"Sure." Most likely he was doing the Herrons a favor of some sort.

At the house, he encouraged her to wait on the porch, then dashed inside. He returned with what appeared to be a picnic basket in one hand and an insulated drink carrier in the other.

She fell into step beside him as he descended the stairs. "Let me guess. Mrs. Herron wants to counter all the sugar she's been feeding Maddy with a healthy supper."

"Could be." Eyes twinkling, he shot her a mischievous grin.

She studied him with a furrowed brow. Was he up to something, and if so, what?

They veered onto a paved pathway leading to a shaded picnic area where Stephanie had spent many quiet evenings. It was one of her favorite locations in the orchard.

She glanced around, expecting to see one of the Herrons with her daughter, but no one else was around.

She faced Caden. "What's this about?"

He offered her a smile that turned her insides to mush, then proceeded to the picnic table beneath the shade of a towering pecan tree.

Stepping closer, she watched as he started unloading the contents of his containers. Cold soft drink bottles with beads of condensation sliding down the plastic. Tea sandwiches, carrot and celery slices, what looked like dip of some sort and...chocolate-covered strawberries.

"I hope you're hungry." Last of the items unpacked, he motioned for her to sit.

She obliged, feeling suddenly shy. "You did all this?" *For me?*

He shrugged. "I had some help. From Mrs. Herron and your princess."

She laughed, envisioning Maddy dipping strawberries in chocolate, her face and hands even stickier than they'd been from the snow cone. "I imagine she helped taste everything, as well."

"As every culinary artist should." He winked, accelerating her pulse, then sat beside her.

When had he planned all this? Before his call from the sheriff? She hoped so, because that would mean he'd believed in her innocence on his own.

She needed that to be true.

"Stephanie." He angled toward her so that their knees touched. "I'm so sorry I doubted you, even for a second, and that was all. Only for a fraction of a moment. But then my brain caught up, and I realized there was no way you could've had anything to do with the drug theft or anything remotely criminal."

"I want to believe you. But if you hold even the slightest distrust... I'm not sure my heart could take it."

"I understand completely. I wish I could rewind that whole day. Wish I would've given myself more time to think things through. I know I hurt you, and I'm sorry. But I also want you to know that I plan on sticking by your side, if you'll let me."

"I'm more concerned with what might happen if we build a relationship and you don't trust me."

"Because of what you experienced with John—you're worried I might become possessive and suspicious?"

She nodded and dropped her gaze.

He cupped her chin in his warm, strong hand and gently raised it until her eyes met his. "I want you to feel safe with me, Stephanie. I plan on doing everything I can to make sure you do. And I'll never hurt you. You have to believe that."

"I want to." A tear slipped down her cheek.

He thumbed it away. "If you'll let me, I'll spend my last breath doing all I can to see that you and Maddy are protected and well cared for. Let me earn your trust."

She gave a wobbly laugh. Caden wasn't the only one with trust issues. "I guess we'll just have to learn together, huh? According to Mrs. Herron, that's what relationships are all about. Growing closer to each other until all those doubts and questions formed during painful pasts are erased completely."

Maybe that was part of the two becoming one, complete, like the Bible talked about.

"Yeah?" He grinned, and for a moment, she thought he was going to give a whoop.

She smiled. "Yeah."

Still grinning, he opened a napkin first in front of Stephanie and then in front of himself and placed sandwich triangles on each. "You up for walking some trails?"

She glanced at the time on her phone. "Shouldn't we be getting back?"

"Faith and her friends have the booth covered."

"How long have you been planning this?"

He shrugged and popped a strawberry into his mouth. "Long enough to take away all your excuses."

She laughed. The fact that he'd gone through such trouble, that he'd sacrifice the free networking opportunity this festival provided, touched her more than she could express. "Well, when you put it that way…"

"Is that a yes?"

The tender adoration in his eyes melted her insides. "That's a yes." She couldn't remember the last time a man had made her feel so cherished.

After lunch, he deposited their remaining picnic items back at the Herrons', then led Stephanie past a field of coneflowers to a trail she hadn't yet explored. As the entered the treed area bordering the south side of the property, the temperature dropped a good ten degrees. A soft breeze rustled the leaves, carrying with it the rich scent of earth.

He twined his fingers through hers. "I've been wanting to talk to you about something."

"Yes?"

"After your internship…are you still wanting to stay on at the clinic? Full time?"

Her heart skipped a beat. Was he about to offer her a job? Trying to maintain a level of professionalism, she took in a deep breath and released it slowly. "I would." She frowned. "But what if—?"

"You decide you're done with me?" He chuckled, then his gaze intensified. "I don't plan on letting that happen. But if you do, your position stays. Your employment is in no way connected to this." He raised their intertwined hands.

"Thanks for saying that." For reading her unspoken concerns.

With a slight nod, he explained some new business he'd soon be receiving, his plans for the vet he'd recently hired, and her part in the clinic's anticipated growth. "We should probably talk salary. But not now. Maybe over lunch tomorrow. I don't want to ruin this moment."

Her heart swelled to think their time together meant as much to him as it did to her.

She smiled, then halted mid-step.

He turned to look at her. "What is it?"

"I just realized how pleasant this is. Being here. With you." That was the gist of it, and yet, that truth carried more depth than she could possibly explain. She'd never felt this way with John.

Caden pulled her close. "I feel the same way."

He wrapped his strong arm around her back, and his eyes dropped to her mouth.

Her breath hitched as he leaned closer, then brushed his lips against hers, feathery soft, tentative at first. But then she leaned into him, and he deepened his kiss.

She melted against him, all of her insecurities gone.

She had no doubt she could trust this man—with her heart and her daughter.

Epilogue

One year later

Stephanie stepped out of her car and breathed in the summer air, fresh and crisp after a midafternoon rain. She surveyed her surroundings with a smile. The tall grass splashed with red, purple and yellow wildflowers. The wisps of clouds that slowly drifted across the blue sky.

"Mama! I want out!"

Laughing, she dashed toward the back seat, where her daughter had freed herself from her booster and was fussing to get out. She opened Maddy's door and helped her slide to her feet. "Sorry, peanut."

She'd barely finished her sentence before Maddy had dashed toward the Stoughtons' house and was scampering up the stairs. She acted the same way at Caden's childhood home as she did when they went to his place for dinner. She loved all the Stoughtons.

As did Stephanie, though she loved the youngest sibling most.

She reached the stoop as Maddy was ringing the bell. Again and again.

"Okay." She placed her hand over Maddy's. "They heard you."

A moment later, Mrs. Stoughton answered the door dressed in a red blouse and white capris. "Well, now, if it isn't my favorite four-year-old." She swooped down, snatched Maddy off her feet, squeezed her into a tight hug that made her giggle, then set her down.

The house smelled like smoked meat and yeasty rolls. "Thanks for inviting us over."

"Actually, that was Caden. And he has no intention of sharing you with us all." She winked.

"I'm sorry. I thought we were eating here."

A mischievous glint lit Mrs. Stoughton's eyes. "Oh, you are. At the gazebo. But Mr. Stoughton and I weren't invited."

"Oh." She stood there for a moment, trying to make sense of what she was saying. Then she smiled. "Let me guess. A picnic." For a man who spent most of his time with big, stinky animals, Caden sure could be romantic. But what about Maddy? Should she not have brought her? She glanced down at her daughter.

"Little miss is invited."

Stephanie's smile returned. "Thanks." While she and Caden had enjoyed numerous dates alone, she loved how often he included Maddy. And not merely for Stephanie's sake or to "make an effort." He obviously adored her.

If ever Stephanie could choose a daddy for her girl, Caden would be it.

The past year had felt a bit like a dream.

"Alright, peanut. Let's go see what Mr. Caden is up to."

"Yeah!" She spun around, scanned the flower-dotted grasslands, then took off toward their most-often followed path.

Stephanie hurried to catch up, reaching her at the tire swing.

Maddy stopped and looked about with a frown.

Stephanie grabbed her hand. "A little farther, sweet pea."

They continued toward the gazebo, Stephanie increasing her pace to match Maddy's part-skipping, part-walking gait while she chatted about everything from the white honey boxes reflecting the sun in the distance to the horse stables in the east.

Stephanie ruffled her hair. "Maybe we can go riding after supper."

"Yay!" Maddy jumped, which turned into continuous hopping.

Laughing, Stephanie followed with a slight bounce in her step, as well.

When they reached the gazebo, Caden stood to greet them. He wore his favorite cowboy hat and boots but had traded his usual snug T-shirt and faded jeans for a new-looking pair and button-down shirt.

"Hi." He shot her a boyish grin, then turned to Maddy. "My little buddy!" He picked her up beneath her armpits, swung her in the air, then dropped her back on her feet. He faced Stephanie. "Hope y'all are hungry." He led the way up the gazebo steps.

Stephanie's eyes widened as she surveyed the table. She hadn't expected a tablecloth at all, or a picnic, for that matter, but lace, with actual dishes? In the center was a bouquet of wildflowers, likely handpicked. "Wow. I don't know what to say."

He pulled her chair out for her. "I wanted tonight to be memorable."

She studied him. "Wait. It's been a year since we first started dating."

"To the day."

"You're so sweet to remember."

"And you're so sweet to forget and let me have the fun of surprising you."

"You like that, huh? Because I can, and probably will, do a lot more forgetting, I'm sure."

"Counting on it." He winked, helped Maddy into her chair, which he'd padded with a pillow to help her reach, then sat beside her and across from Stephanie.

"I don't deserve you, Caden Stoughton."

"I'd say you've got that backward." He dished food onto her plate. "But then, I'd rather not help you come to your senses. I'm still amazed at how God brought us together."

"Kept me in Sage Creek, you mean?"

Though she'd been teasing, his expression turned serious. "Exactly. Keeping me from making the biggest mistake of my life." He stood. "I was going to wait until after supper, but…" He stood and pulled a small velvet box from the picnic basket.

"Caden, what are you doing?"

He turned to Maddy and dropped to one knee before her. "Maddy, girl, you know I love you more than cotton candy, ice cream and beef brisket combined, right?"

She stopped playing with her silverware, which she'd apparently imagined as people, and nodded.

"Think it might be okay if I stick around for a while?"

"Uh-huh."

"Like…forever?"

"Yep." She thrust her hand into her water glass and fished around for an ice cube, which she promptly shoved into her mouth.

He laughed. "Good to hear."

He turned to Stephanie, and the intensity in his eyes accelerated her pulse. "You're the most beautiful woman in all of Texas, and I'm not talking just about your looks. You're kind, so very strong and an amazing mother. I love watching you with Maddy—the way your face lights up the minute she says your name. I love how patient and gentle you are with every animal that comes into our clinic. But mostly, I love how you make me feel. Somehow your hope, your zeal for life, is contagious."

He took a deep breath and wiped a hand on his jeans. "Here's hoping I don't butcher the most important question of my life." He opened the velvet box to reveal a glimmering diamond set in a golden vine-motif band. "This was my great-aunt's engagement ring. Mama's been saving it for me."

Her heart squeezed. "Oh, Caden."

"Stephanie, before you came to town, I was content to live my quiet, solitary life. I'd convinced myself I was happy, with just me, my dogs, my practice and all the animals God saw fit to bring my way. But then I met you, and you captured my attention and my heart immediately. I tried to fight it. I kept telling myself all the reasons I couldn't fall for you, but my heart wouldn't listen. So here I am, telling you that I don't want to live a day without you or Maddy-girl."

He took her hand in his. "I love you, more than I thought possible to love a woman. Stephanie Thornton, will you marry me?" He slipped the ring on her trembling finger.

She gave a squeal. She didn't even have to consider her answer. God truly was giving her a second chance—at life and at love. "Yes. Oh, Caden, yes. A thousand times yes."

"Yeah!" He sprang to his feet, pulling her to hers, as well. "You've made me one happy man." He spun her around. Then, breathing hard, he planted her back on her feet, cupped her face in his hands and kissed her with a love so strong, it nearly buckled her knees. As she melted into his embrace, a surge of joy exploded within her. A joy she used to be afraid to even hope for.

Not anymore. Because now she actually believed that

she was not only worthy of love but had actually found it. She'd endured a long, hard three years, but here in Caden's strong arms, every tear she'd cried leading to this moment felt like little more than a distant memory.

* * * * *

*If you enjoyed this story,
look for Jennifer Slattery's earlier books*

Restoring Her Faith
Hometown Healing
Building a Family
Chasing Her Dream

Available now from Love Inspired!

Find more great reads at www.LoveInspired.com

Dear Reader,

Sometimes threads in our lives emerge that reveal God's
heart and how He wants to express that to the world. Lately,
I've become increasingly aware of the message God has
been writing through the stories He helps me craft, and it's
this: God's love has the power to heal the brokenhearted,
and He often uses His children to do so.

As I was considering what I most wanted to say to you,
I realized this was the thread God had woven through *Her
Small-Town Refuge*, as well. In this Sage Creek romance,
we see the healing impact one man, Caden, can have over
others, including the rescue dogs he took in and Stephanie, the single mom healing from past abuse. This reminds
me of two truths: God wants to heal you and I of all our
past wounds so that we can live completely free, and God
wants to use us to heal others. May we courageously follow His lead in both calls.

If you would like to see the two rescue dogs—my grand-
puppies—that made it into this story (Bella and Rocky),
visit Misha and Buba on Instagram at mish_n_bubs/.

Jennifer Slattery